–The–
Bandit of
Ashley Downs

D1025352

Trailblazer Books

TITLE	HISTORIC CHARACTERS
Attack in the Rye Grass	Marcus & Narcissa Whitman
The Bandit of Ashley Downs	George Müller
The Chimney Sweep's Ransom	John Wesley
Escape from the Slave Traders	David Livingstone
The Hidden Jewel	Amy Carmichael
Imprisoned in the Golden City	Adoniram and Ann Judson
Kidnapped by River Rats	William & Catherine Booth
Listen for the Whippoorwill	Harriet Tubman
The Queen's Smuggler	William Tyndale
Shanghaied to China	Hudson Taylor
Spy for the Night Riders	Doctor Martin Luther
Trial by Poison	Mary Slessor

–The–
Bandit of
Ashley Downs

DAVE & NETA JACKSON

Text Illustrations by
Julian Jackson

BETHANY HOUSE PUBLISHERS
MINNEAPOLIS, MINNESOTA 55438

Inside illustrations by Julian Jackson.
Cover design and illustration by Catherine Reishus McLaughlin.

Published by Bethany House Publishers
A Ministry of Bethany Fellowship, Inc.
11300 Hampshire Avenue South
Minneapolis, Minnesota 55438

Printed in the United States of America

Library of Congress Cataloging-in-Publication Data

Jackson, Dave.
    The bandit of Ashley Downs / Dave & Neta Jackson.
        p. cm. — (Trailblazer Books)
    Summary: With God's love, Curly, a young nineteenth-century English boy convicted of armed robbery, reforms his ways after being sent to one of George Müller's orphan homes.
    [1. Orphans—Fiction.   2. Robbers and outlaws—Fiction. 3. Müller, George, 1805–1898—Fiction. 4. Christian life—Fiction. 5. England—Fiction.] I. Jackson, Neta. II. Title. III. Series.
PZ7.J132418Ban   1993
[Fic]—dc20   92–46182
ISBN 1–55661–270–2   CIP
                                                    AC

George Müller founded an orphanage in Bristol, England, that at first cared for thirty children. By faith, and without going into debt or revealing his financial needs to anyone but God, the orphanage grew until Müller had cared for more than ten thousand children during his lifetime.

The fictional character of Curly Roddy is based on a real boy—William Ready (who was not, however, a bandit). As the story states, William was brought to Ashley Downs in 1872 by James Walk, a city missionary connected with St. George's Church on Bloomsbury Way in London.

All other characters are fictional, but each event at Ashley Downs involving prayer and faith is true.

DAVE AND NETA JACKSON are a husband/wife writing team who have authored or coauthored many books on marriage and family, the church, and relationships, including *On Fire for Christ: Stories from Martyrs Mirror*, the Pet Parables series, and the Caring Parent series.

They have three children: Julian, the illustrator for the Trailblazer series, Rachel, a high school student, and Samantha, their Cambodian foster daughter. They make their home in Evanston, Illinois, where they are active members of Reba Place Church.

CONTENTS

Chapter 1

Escape From the Tower

CURLY RODDY YANKED OPEN the door to the bell tower of St. George's Church and slipped into the pitch dark staircase. The sexton was not likely to look for him here, he hoped. He held his breath and listened for the sound of footsteps.

That morning, the homeless orphan boy had hurried to church early hoping to find someone to pickpocket. Curly was not a mean kid, just hungry and in need of money for food. He had been standing in the busy lobby watching some people collect money for an orphanage when he noticed a woman walk by wearing a light gray shawl. She was carrying her purse very loosely, and Curly was certain he could cut its strings and be off with it without her knowing. He followed, pushing his way through the crowd, intent on catching up with her.

That was when the sexton had spotted him. Young boys from good families didn't dress so shabbily or behave so rudely. And they certainly didn't wear their caps in church, so even though the quiet notes from the great pipe organ urged worshipful silence, the church caretaker had called out, "Hey, you, boy! Come back here." But Curly had ducked down the hallway out of the old man's sight.

Now, hiding in the belfry, he cautiously opened the door a crack and peeked down the hall, uncertain whether the sexton had really noticed him or not. Maybe the old man had called to someone else, and Curly had run unnecessarily.

But no, through the crack he could see the sexton, looking this way and that. The twelve-year-old boy started to pull the door shut, then thought twice about it. Would it be better to get caught and turned over to the police or get locked in the tower? After all, in England, in 1872, unless someone died, a bell tower might remain locked until the following Sunday's bell ringing. *By then, the bells would peal for me*, thought Curly, *'cause I'd be dead.*

The old man stopped and as if by instinct looked directly at the belfry door. Curly could see a wry grin spread across his face as he came toward the boy's hiding-place pulling a ring of jangling keys from his jacket pocket. "Well, well, looks as if the tower's unlocked," he muttered. Curly backed away from the door, deeper into the darkness, certain that the old caretaker would fling the door open and catch him.

Instead, the sexton pushed the door tightly shut and said, "If you're in there, you little thief, then this ought to keep you from picking anyone's pocket for a while." The bolt clacked loudly as it moved in the lock; the rattling keys were pulled from the door. Then the sexton's heels clicked on the stone floor as he walked away down the hall.

Curly had figured stealing from unsuspecting church members was easier than picking the pockets of cautious shoppers in the marketplace, but he had never expected a problem like this. He stood silently, trying to force his eyes to penetrate the darkness, but not even a dim glimmer came from under the door. *How could a place be so black?* he wondered. He groped forward until he found the door handle. Turning it was useless; the door was locked.

Panic rose in Curly's chest, and he began to pound on the door. "Help! Help!" he yelled, but no one responded. After a few minutes he stopped, breathing hard. It was no use. *I must think*, he told himself, trying to calm down. *There's got to be a way to get out of this.* In the eerie silence, he became aware of the deep rumbling tones of the great pipe organ. The service was starting, and people were singing. No wonder no one could hear him banging on the door. *If I'm patient, I may be able to attract someone's attention after the service.*

While he waited, the pinched feeling in Curly's stomach reminded him that he hadn't had anything to eat since the day before. He wondered whether Spuds Baxter, the small-time criminal with whom he stayed, would rescue him. *Not likely*, concluded Curly. *He won't even miss me until I'm not around to be his lookout.*

Finally, Curly decided to do a little exploring. Maybe there was some other way out of the tower. Maybe up higher there would be a door leading to the balcony at the rear of the church. He cautiously shuffled back across the tiny room until his feet bumped into the wooden steps. He reached out to steady himself against the stone wall and then began climbing, counting the steps as he went.

At twelve steps, the staircase turned with the wall and went up another twelve steps. When this had happened four times, Curly figured he had made one full turn around the inside of the tower and must be at least as high as the balcony, but there was no door. *Could it be higher yet?* He moved quickly up another set of steps, but in his haste slammed his head into the heavy planks of the ceiling. The darkness lit up with stars, and he slumped to the steps to recover.

He didn't like to think of how high he was. He could not tell if the center of the stairwell was open all the way to the floor, and in the dark it was hard to keep his balance when he took his hand off the wall. He felt the stone wall more carefully. *I must have missed the door*, he thought. *Why would they build stairs that go right up into the ceiling?*

Curly felt around until he discovered what seemed like a large trap door above him. He pushed, but it wouldn't budge. He turned around and backed up a couple more steps until he could duck his head and set his hunched shoulders against the trap door. By using the strength in his legs, the trap door finally gave way with a loud creak and slowly opened.

The boy climbed out into a dim, dungeon-like room. Light was coming from windows high in the tower through which the sound of the bells rang out over London. The bells hung huge and gaping overhead, much larger than Curly had ever imagined. Hanging from each bell was a long rope tied off to a peg along the wall.

Curly looked around. Up one wall ran a ladder. *They must climb that if they need to fix the bells*, he thought. Hanging neatly from pegs along another wall were several extra coils of rope, some thick—some thin.

Suddenly, Curly had an idea: *If I had a long enough rope, I could climb that ladder and lower myself down from the belfry window*. He removed his cap for a moment and pushed his curly hair—for which he was named—back off his sweaty forehead. He was a good acrobat and sometimes earned money doing tricks in the pubs, but the idea of climbing down the outside of a bell tower with a rope, like a spider suspended from its web, seemed impossible. Still, what other choice did he have? It was either try that or get caught when the sexton opened the door. Or die of thirst.

He selected a large coil of the thin rope, looped it over his head and shoulders, and began climbing the ladder. Halfway up, Curly pulled on a rung that suddenly broke loose. The jerk nearly toppled him as he clutched at the side of the ladder. Regaining his hold and balance, he glanced down just as the broken rung hit the floor far below. He might have gone down with it if he hadn't been hanging on so tightly with his other hand. The scare caused Curly's legs to shake, and he hardly had the strength to pull himself up across the gap where the rung was missing. From then on, he tested each rung before trusting his full weight to it.

Finally, reaching the top of the ladder, a terrible noise erupted above Curly's head. Seven pigeons took off from the bell timbers and flew out the belfry windows. The shock left the boy's heart slugging the inside of his chest. *How did I get myself into this mess?* he wondered as he dragged himself up on the heavy timbers that supported the huge bells and looked out over London.

Years of coal smoke had turned them nearly black. Heavy gray clouds—nearly as dark—hung so low that Curly felt as if he could reach out and touch them. He worked his way around to the front of the tower and looked down on the busy street of Bloomsbury Way, some sixty feet below. He felt a little dizzy and thought he might faint. From this side, people would surely see him.

The best way, he decided, was to go out the northeast side of the belfry and drop down to the church roof—about fifteen feet was Curly's guess.

Surrounding the belfry and partially hiding the bell windows were stone columns, small copies of the six giant columns across the front of the church, which created a porch similar to that on a Greek temple. Curly tied one end of the rope to one of the small columns outside the northeast belfry window and flung the rest down onto the church roof. Carefully the boy climbed out onto the sill between two columns, then, turning to lie on his stomach, he let his feet hang down the side of the tower until they reached a small ledge.

When he was balanced, he grabbed the rope and began to work his way farther down. At about six feet, he came to another ledge and took a break. Looking down at the church roof, he tried to figure out how he would get from the church roof to the ground.

Suddenly, he realized there might not be a way if he didn't have a long rope, and the one he was using was tied securely to the pillar above.

A damp breeze made Curly shiver as he tried to think. It was starting to sprinkle. *I need to go back for another rope. It's the only way*, he thought. He tried to climb back up the rope, but his arms were so tired that he could barely make it. When he finally grasped the sill again and was about to pull himself back inside, he thought of another solution.

The rain was coming harder as he untied the rope from the smooth, round column and retied it around his body under his arms. Then he looped the other end around the column as though it were a pulley and, by letting the rope out hand over hand, he lowered himself slowly down. Inch by inch, foot by foot he worked his way down the stone tower.

When the boy reached the church roof, he released the end of the rope and pulled it free of the column. When it came falling down in a heap beside him, Curly felt proud of himself: Now he had a rope to lower himself from the roof to the ground.

He turned and walked toward the back of the church, looking for the best place to get down. The roof wasn't steep, but the rain mixed with soot was making it very slick. He had no sooner realized this when his feet skidded out from under him and he began to slide.

Flipping quickly to his stomach, he clawed for a grip, but the surface was too slick. The closer he came to the edge, the more certain he was that the forty-foot fall to the ground would mean certain death. His fingernails tore until they bled as he tried to dig them into a shingle to slow himself down.

Then, *clank!* His feet dropped over the edge. For an instant one toe caught in the gutter, but then it popped loose. The other toe didn't even catch, and his feet and legs shot out into space. But just as he was about to pitch over the edge, his body was yanked to a painful stop.

The other end of the rope that was still tied around his body had become wedged between two stones up at the corner of the belfry tower. It had saved his life.

Carefully, Curly pulled himself back up onto the roof and lay very still, plastered to the edge, his toes firmly planted in the gutter. He was too frightened to move, let alone to look down.

How long he lay there, he did not know, but finally he realized he had to do something. He looked both ways and noticed a vent pipe sticking up toward the back of the church, very near the edge of the roof. *If I can get back there*, he thought, *and tie my rope onto that pipe, I might be able to lower myself to the ground.*

He whipped the rope up and down a couple times until it came free from the tower stones where it was wedged. Then he inched himself sideways like a crab along the edge of the roof: one foot out, tuck it in the gutter, slide sideways, then bring the other foot along. It was slow going, but he made progress, and by the time he reached the pipe it had stopped raining.

It didn't take Curly long to tie one end of the rope around the pipe and throw the other end over the edge. Good; it reached the ground. But in watching it fall, he started to feel dizzy again. *I better not look down again*, he thought.

It took all the courage the boy could muster to ease himself over the edge and begin working his way down the side of the building. Every so often a window sill or ledge gave him enough of a toehold to take a break, but he was careful not to look down.

His feet touched the damp ground just as the church organ peeled out the closing hymn of the service. He sank to the earth, leaning his back against the stone church. His legs were too weak to move.

The excitement of his escape would have been enough for the average kid, but Curly wasn't average. Having lived on the streets for the past six years, he had faced many frightening experiences. Survival demanded that he keep moving, and his stomach reminded him again of how empty it was. Shakily, he got to his feet, wiped off some of the black grime, pulled his cap low over his eyes, and walked around to the front of the church.

If that woman with the gray shawl comes out carrying her purse like she did when she went in, he thought, *I'm still gonna get me some lunch money.*

He waited across the street from the church as the people poured out of the doors, and sure enough, the woman in the gray shawl was among them, only now she had a young girl by her side. *Don't matter,* thought Curly. *I'll still snatch her purse.* Staying close enough to keep them in sight, but not so close as to draw attention to himself, Curly followed along Bloomsbury Way until the pair was away from the Sunday crowd, then he snuck up right behind them, ready to make his move.

It was then that he noticed the woman's clothes were patched. This was no wealthy matron, and her companion was similarly tattered. The girl looked to be about ten—the same age as Curly's younger sister. When she turned to say something to the woman, Curly got a real shock. *Why, she looks just like my sister!* he thought. Of course he hadn't seen his sister for six years, but this girl had the same wavy blonde hair and the same little pug nose—and dark brown eyes. *Ain't many gals have brown eyes with yellow hair*, thought Curly, his heart thumping strangely. Most girls with blonde hair had blue eyes. Could it . . . could she be his sister?

He hung back, but kept following the pair as they turned a corner into a narrow street.

Chapter 2

A Ripe Opportunity

CURLY TRAILED THE GRAY SHAWLED WOMAN and the little girl for three more blocks, as the houses got smaller and shabbier. Then he overheard the girl say, "Mama, when is Papa coming back from sea?"

"By Christmas, God willing," the woman said, putting her arm gently around the child's shoulder.

That answered it. The girl couldn't be Curly's sister. His father and mother had both died, leaving him and his nine sisters and brothers orphans. Curly wasn't sad about his father's death. He had been a mean drunk most of the time, beating his siblings and even his mother. But when his mother died . . . Curly felt like his heart had been cut out.

Grudging neighbors had taken in the younger children while the older ones had been sent to workhouses where they were forced to work twelve or fourteen hours a day. The last Curly heard, the older ones had all run away from the workhouses, and his younger brothers and sisters had been moved around so often that he no longer knew where they were. The butcher's wife had taken him in, but the butcher was as mean as his father and beat Curly nearly every day. Finally, the boy ran away to London, where he'd been living on the streets ever since.

Sometimes he slept in trash bins; sometimes he sneaked into a stable and nestled in the warm hay. But lately he had found a place in a warehouse where Spuds Baxter, a petty criminal, was a watchman.

Curly stopped and watched as the woman and little girl slipped away from him. If she had a father and mother, she couldn't be his sister. Still . . . the girl reminded him of his sister, and the family was obviously poor. Even though his stomach was cramping with hunger pains, he decided against snatching the woman's purse.

Not knowing what else to do, he turned back toward the warehouse, but an unfamiliar pub caught his attention. The sign above the door displayed a picture of a man drawing a longbow and some words Curly couldn't read. Music and laughter spilled out the open door, drawing Curly inside. Maybe he could earn a penny here.

"Hey, mister," he said to a man sitting at a table with a pretty woman beside him, "you want to see a trick?"

"Get out of here, kid," the man snapped. "You got soot all down the front o' you."

Curly did a neat back flip and made a little bow. He had learned that even when a person wasn't interested, one quick trick could attract attention. And if there was a pretty woman at hand—young women were always impressed—the man would not want to appear a cheapskate.

"Oh, my," the woman said, smiling at Curly.

"Not bad, lad," the man said grudgingly. "Bet you can't do three in a row."

"For a penny, I'll try." Though he could do it easily, Curly knew that if he was too confident, people wouldn't pay until he got to his hardest tricks.

"Half-penny, but only if you make it."

Curly did the three back flips, and the woman jumped up and clapped. "Stand back, there," the man ordered as Curly held out his hand. "You'll get soot all over the lady." He fished a coin out and dropped it in Curly's hand. Curly was ready to volunteer to walk around the room on his hands when someone grabbed him from behind and spun him around.

Smack.

A flash went off inside Curly's head and pain stabbed through his face. Someone had just slugged him in the nose, but tears came so quickly to Curly's eyes, he couldn't even bring the person into focus.

"The only way an outsider puts on a show in here is if he fights me," a menacing voice said. Curly blinked and then saw a kid a head taller than him standing in a boxer's stance. "So, put up your fists, or get out," the challenger sneered.

Seeing he was outmatched, Curly backed off and quickly ran out of the pub.

The small coin he still clutched in his hand bought him a muffin and a piece of taffy for his lunch. But the food didn't ease the sad feeling inside. Curly wandered back to the warehouse. Things weren't going well.

Spuds Baxter yelled at him when he entered the warehouse, "Where've you been? I needed somebody to keep a lookout for me. I had customers this morning."

Spuds' "customers" were thieves like himself. The warehouse owners had hired Spuds to live there and prevent people from stealing the merchandise. "I'm a good watchman," Spuds had once boasted to Curly. "Been here three years, and no one has broken in and carried off a wagonload of merchandise."

That was actually true, but Spuds stole small amounts himself to sell to *his* customers, who resold it on the black market. Curly's job as lookout was to make sure none of the merchants who stored things legally in the warehouse came by when Spuds was dealing with his black market customers.

"If I don't take too much," Spuds had explained proudly, "no 'un notices. There's always some breakage and loss during shipping, so who's gonna reweigh a fifty-pound sack of chocolate to find out that a couple pounds are missing?"

Now Spuds frowned as he looked Curly up and

down. "What happened to you?" he growled. Spuds had gotten his nickname from his rough, pockmarked face and large, bulbous nose that made him look like a red potato. "I thought you slept here last night, but you look like you slept in a coal bin. Get outta here . . . and don't come back till you clean up. You attract too much attention when you're that filthy."

The muddy soot from the church roof had dried enough so that Curly was able to get rid of most of it with an old horse brush. Then he stripped to the waist, took a broken bar of lye soap, and washed thoroughly in the rain barrel behind the warehouse. When he finished, the blond highlights were noticeable again in his curly brown hair.

Wet and shivering in the cold afternoon air as he put his shirt and coat back on, the boy suddenly remembered what he meant to tell Spuds. With all the worry of getting locked in the bell tower and nearly dying, he had completely forgotten something he'd seen when he had first entered the church that morning . . . even before he saw the woman in the gray shawl.

"Hey, Spuds," he yelled, running back inside the warehouse. "I got an idea."

"Now you look human," Spuds said as he puffed on his pipe beside the little stove. "So what's your idea?"

"When I went to church this morning—"

"Church?" Spuds guffawed. "What were you doing at church?"

"You know I go to church. It's a good place to pick up some extra change. Anyway, as I was going in, there were two people standing there in the church lobby collecting money. I hung around thinking they might drop some money on the floor."

"More likely, you were trying to see where people kept their money so you could pickpocket them," Spuds smirked.

"So? What if I was?" Curly shrugged. "Anyway, I got this idea. They're trying to raise three thousand pounds in hard cash to send to an orphan house—in Bristol, I think. But . . . what if we was to rob it on the way?"

Smoke billowed out of Spuds' pipe. "What if we . . . *what*? Do you know what you're talking about, boy?"

"Yeah. I'm talking about *three thousand pounds*. That's more money than you or I'll ever see in our lifetime."

"An' just how are we gonna pinch it?"

"You know. Like highway bandits."

"Highway bandits? Are you crazy, kid? Bandits end up shot or in prison or swinging from a rope. Nah. Not me. That kind of work's too dangerous."

Spuds sat there puffing hard on his pipe and staring at the stove. His curiosity was obviously running high. Finally, he said, "So, when are they supposed to deliver this money?"

"I dunno," said Curly. "But I heard someone say they're gonna have a big celebration at St. George's next Sunday to 'bless' the money."

Spuds just puffed silently. "No fool would carry that much cash all the way to Bristol," he said with finality as he got up and knocked the ash out his pipe on the palm of his hand. "The only way they'd send that kind of money is with a bank transfer."

"Well, maybe we could rob it at the church," said Curly, hopefully. Three thousand pounds was a lot of money and he wasn't about to give up easily.

"Hey. Robbin' ain't like thievin'. They're gonna have armed guards for sure. Besides, I might snitch a little here and there to make a livin', but I'm no big-time criminal. I got my pride."

"You got a gun," said Curly.

"Wha—? How'd you know about that?"

"I seen you cleaning it once," Curly said casually. What he had actually seen was Spuds removing a large, loose stone from the wall behind his bunk. From a secret space behind where the stone had fit, the older man took out a pistol and a small money box. He had then replaced the money box and the stone and set about cleaning the gun. But Curly didn't dare reveal that he knew about the hiding place; Spuds was sure to get angry.

"Well, it's just for protection," Spuds muttered nervously. "A man needs protection sometimes, you understand? But I've never robbed anyone with it."

✧ ✧ ✧ ✧

The next Sunday, Curly made his way back to St. George's Church. He wasn't sure if he went to see the girl who looked like his sister, or if he went to look for people to pickpocket, or to find out more about the money for the orphan house. Maybe all three. But when he got there, no one was standing in the church lobby collecting funds for the orphans like they'd been the last Sunday. *Maybe Spuds was right*, thought Curly. *Maybe there's no way to rob the church of the special collection.*

He felt let down. All week he had been dreaming about that money. If people were so eager to give to orphans, then he certainly was entitled to some of it. After all, he was an orphan and had been forced to live a pretty rough life because of it.

Curly found a seat in the back of the church, keeping an eye on the sexton, but the old caretaker didn't seem to recognize him.

The boy sat patiently as the music from the big pipe organ filled the big church, drowning out people's voices. After the singing, a man stood up. Curly recognized him as one of the men who had been collecting money the week before. "I am happy to say we have reached our goal of three thousand pounds for George Müller's orphan house," he announced. "Mr. Walk, I want you to come up here to the front so everyone can get a good look at you."

Curly stared at the tall man with slightly hunched shoulders who walked toward the front carrying a black satchel. "This is James Walk," the first man continued, "chairman of our charity committee. Bright and early Tuesday morning he is going to board a coach right out here—from our own church step—and travel to Bristol to deliver our contributions.

"It's all right here, folks. Open it up, James. Open it up," he said, gesturing toward the small black case. James Walk opened the case, and the speaker reached in. With one hand he held up a stack of banded bills, while with the other he lifted a small but heavy looking sack above his head. Even from the back of the church, Curly could hear the jingle of silver and gold coins within the bag.

"Let's pray Godspeed to Mr. Walk, and that this money would genuinely help some deserving orphans." With that the man launched into a long prayer. But Curly wasn't bored. He was thinking about all that money. *No more pickpocketing, no more tricks in pubs, no . . .*

A few hours later, when Curly told Spuds about what he'd heard at St. George's, Spuds listened with more interest. "Now, when did they say Walk was leaving?" he asked again, and Curly told him. "Going to Bristol, is he?"

Curly nodded.

"Hmm. Only one good road to Bristol this time o' year," said Spuds, puffing on his pipe. "And there's one stretch not too far out o' town where we might be able to stop a coach."

Excitement pounded in Curly's ears. Was Spuds willing to consider a robbery after all? But he said nothing, just watched the older man walk back and forth, frowning and puffing. The boy knew better than to interrupt Spuds' thoughts.

"It's not the public stagecoach, is it?" Spuds asked.

"I don't think so," said Curly. "The public stage would never make a private stop at the church."

"Anyone else going with him?"

"No, just Mr. Walk."

"Hmm. That means Walk, a driver, maybe a coachman—three. I ought to be able to take three people if Jake and Shorty would help."

"And me," put in Curly.

"No, not a kid," said Spuds as he spat into a corner. "I'd never take a kid on a job like this."

"But . . . it was my idea!" protested Curly. "I deserve a cut."

"Calm down. We'll cut you in, don't worry about that. But I'm not gonna make a bandit out o' you."

"But you gotta take me! I . . . I—" Curly struggled for a convincing reason. "I'm the only one who knows what Mr. Walk looks like," he blurted out. "What if you tried to rob the wrong person?"

Spuds got up and walked to the small door in the back of the warehouse. "You can just describe him to me. There can't be that many coaches traveling the road to Bristol early in the morning. What's the man look like?"

"Come on, Spuds," Curly pleaded. "You gotta take me."

"Out with it. What's he look like?"

The boy pouted, but finally said, "He's tall . . . thin . . . has dark hair."

"How old is he?"

"I dunno. He's not old."

"Yeah. That describes about a quarter of the men in London. Can't you do better than that?"

"I can do better if you take me. I'll know him when I see him—no mistake about that."

Spuds looked at the boy a long time. Finally, a grin spread over his pockmarked face. "All right. I'll see what Jake and Shorty say."

Chapter 3

Highway Robbery

I F YOU CAN'T KEEP UP, just head on back to London,"
barked Spuds when Curly slipped on the ice.

But Curly *was* keeping up. He was even ahead of
Shorty as the four bandits trudged along the road
from London to Bristol in the middle of the night. *It
must be the weather*, thought Curly. *It's making him
nervous.*

The weather had turned bad. First there had
been a blowing, freezing rain that had stuck to the
trees and bushes. Then, when the wind calmed down,
a light, wispy snow started to fall. It was so dark that
Curly couldn't really see the snow, but the flakes
tickled when they landed on his nose or eyebrows,
and now they had started to cover the ground.

Hiking along the muddy road had become treacherous. The tops of the ruts were frozen and slick with a thin cover of ice and snow, but the bottoms of the deep ruts were still soft mud that stuck to their boots. More than once each of the four travelers had slid into a rut and lost his balance.

Just then the man named Jake slipped and went down, splashing muddy water from the bottom of a rut. He swore harshly. "Mud all over my face," he complained. "This ain't no good. We'll never be able to set up an ambush in the dark. Why don't we wait till it gets light?"

"'Cause we don't want some farmer seeing us walking along this road," growled Spuds. "I didn't plan this foul weather, but by gum, I ain't turning back now 'cause of a little misery. You a quitter, Jake?"

"You know I ain't no quitter, but this is a lot of work for who knows what. We're not even sure there's gonna be three thousand pounds on that coach."

"We don't even know that there'll be a coach from London to Bristol today," added Shorty.

"I told you, St. George's made a big deal about sending James Walk off in the morning," said Curly.

"Just the word of a kid," snarled Shorty. "Got us on a wild goose chase, I'm a-thinkin'."

Then Curly noticed that a patch in the dark sky was getting light enough to see the swirling, wind-blown clouds. *It can't be dawn yet,* he thought. *Besides, that light patch is too high up to be the rising sun.* As they plodded on, the clouds broke and a large moon shone through, turning the whole countryside into a mysterious maze of black and white. It took Curly a few moments to realize that the black shapes were trees and bushes and stone fences, while the white areas were open ground with a fresh dusting of snow.

An hour later the sky had fully cleared and the first hint of dawn was cracking the eastern horizon. The moon had seemed to grow smaller as they'd tramped mile after mile. "This'll do," announced Spuds. They were about ten miles out of London in a wooded, slightly hilly area, far from any farms. Curly felt like this was another world—so quiet and peaceful.

The little band stamped their cold feet and blew on their fingers as Spuds outlined the plan. "We've only got one gun so, Jake and Shorty, don't let anyone see you, especially not the coachman or the driver. They gotta think you have guns, even though you don't. So you two hide on the right side of the road, back there in those bushes.

"Curly. You hide behind that big rock on this side of the road. When the coach gets to the top of this little hill, it'll be going slower because of the pull. You listening? Now, when the coach gets about here . . . you jump out in the middle of the road, waving your arms like you're in trouble and need help."

"What if the driver doesn't stop and runs me over?" objected Curly.

Jake and Shorty snorted.

"Where'd you say this money's coming from?" asked Spuds sarcastically.

"St. George's Church."

"Well, do you think good, God-fearin' church people are going to run down a helpless lad in the middle of the road?"

"No. I guess not." The thought crossed Curly's mind that if he could depend on these church people to be so "good," maybe he shouldn't be stealing from them. But it was too late to worry about that now.

"Now, once that coach stops, you grab the reins of the left horse—the left lead horse if there are four—and hold on tight. Once the driver sees me, he'll know we're up to no good and may try to make a break for it. But you gotta hold that lead horse steady."

Spuds turned to the other two men. "The moment the coach stops, I'll come out waving my gun announcing a holdup. The driver and the coachman will have their attention on me, but the coachman is liable to have a gun, so you two come up behind him and yell, 'Don't move, and don't turn around, or we'll shoot.' Both of you yell loud and clear—and don't stand together."

"What's the point of all this, Spuds?" whined Shorty. "You act like you're directing some fancy-pants play in a theater."

"That's exactly what I'm doing," Spuds snapped. "We got us only one gun—a single-shot pistol at that—but you gotta make them think they're surrounded by armed men. If you don't, that coachman is liable to make a move on us, and somebody could get killed."

35

"Well, I don't want no bloodshed," said Jake. "This highway robbery business is way out of my league as it is. Me, I'm a good burglar, but armed robbery could get us sent to prison for a long time. And don't go shooting anyone, or they'll hang us for sure if we get caught."

"I ain't gonna shoot nobody," said Spuds. "Just do what I say, and nothin'll go wrong."

"But what if there ain't no three thousand pounds of cash on that coach?" said Jake.

"Anyone hiring a private coach has gotta be wealthy enough to have a few trinkets worth taking."

"But not worth going to prison for," Jake muttered.

"Jake, you wouldn't be turnin' yellow, now, would ya? We're all in this together, even the kid. But if you want out, now's the time to scram. Go on, get out of here. We don't need you."

Jake looked at Shorty, then back at Spuds. "Naw. I'm in with you," he said with a shrug.

"All right. Let's get in our positions."

An hour later, Curly was freezing, but still no coach had come along. When the wind blew, the ice on the limbs of the trees crackled and snapped. Each little twig was wrapped in a silver cocoon that sparkled in the growing dawn. They were surrounded by a frozen fairyland, and Curly tried to take his mind off the cold by watching the sparrows harvesting the last seeds from the dried weeds that stuck up out of the inch of snow on the ground.

Then suddenly he heard something coming. From behind the rock where he was hiding, he could not see back down the hill toward London. But from that direction, it sounded like a coach was coming—awfully slowly. The hill hadn't seemed that steep. As the plodding hoofbeats and creaking wheels approached, Curly was just about to jump out when he peeked over the top of the rock and saw that it wasn't a coach at all.

It was a farmer's milk cart.

Curly hunkered back down behind the rock, his heart beating wildly. *That was close*, he thought. *A good thing I didn't jump out. That farmer would've wanted to know who I was . . . probably would've made me get in his cart and go with him.* What worried the boy even more was the thought that the farmer might have figured out something was wrong and gone for help.

If that had happened, it would have ruined the whole plan. And three grown men would have him to blame.

The excitement had not helped Curly warm up. Instead, he was now shivering uncontrollably. He tried to wiggle his feet to get the circulation going, and he pulled his ragged coat closer around himself, but the shivering wouldn't stop.

Then he heard something else coming up the road. This time it sounded more like coach horses trotting along at a fast pace. He heard them splash through the puddles at the bottom of the rise. As the coach started up the hill, a horse snorted, and Curly could hear the harness creaking and the iron rims of carriage wheels striking stones in the road.

And just as Spuds had said, when the coach approached the top of the rise, the beat of the horses' hooves got slower and slower.

This was the moment.

Curly poked his head up and saw two horses just thirty feet away pulling a black coach, its running lights still twinkling in the early morning dawn. He ran out in the road waving his arms and shouting for the driver to stop. The horses set their feet and went back almost on their haunches as they skidded in the muddy ruts while the driver hauled back on the reins and stepped hard on the brake.

Wheezing and snorting, the horses and rig came to a halt a few feet from Curly. Steam was boiling off the horses as Curly reached up and grabbed the reins of the lead horse, but the moment he touched the reins, the beast spooked and reared up on its hind legs. The boy hung on like a fish being pulled from a pond. In a moment he came crashing back down, but the horse continued to pull away, rolling its eyes and yanking its head back again and again. Curly was being whipped around so badly it was all he could do to keep hold of the reins that were cutting into his nearly frozen hands.

In all the excitement, he had no idea if Spuds and the other two bandits had made their appearance

until he heard Spuds yelling, "Come on, get out of there. This is a stick up, so get out of there right now, and keep your hands up!"

Finally, the horse calmed down, and Curly looked back at the coach to see a tall man in a well-tailored coat and black top hat step from the coach with his hands raised. It was James Walk. "That's him," yelled Curly. The man turned and looked at Curly, and a strange look came over his face.

"Where's the money?" Spuds demanded, but the man continued to stare at Curly as if he recognized him. *What if he saw me at church?* worried the boy.

"Come on. Gimme that money," ordered Spuds.

Finally, the man turned his attention back to Spuds and reached carefully into the inside breast pocket of his coat, bringing out a thin wallet. "Not that!" shouted Spuds, but he grabbed it out of the man's hand all the same.

"Well, what do you want, then?" asked Mr. Walk.

"The money you're transporting to Bristol. Come on, come on, now. I don't want to have to use this." He waved the pistol in the man's face, and then yelled back to Jake and Shorty. "You men keep your aim on that coachman. Don't let him make a move. Now, get in there," he said, giving Mr. Walk a shove, "and come out with that shipment of money—and you better not bring a weapon out with you."

Seeing he had no alternative, James Walk turned slowly and climbed back into the coach. In a moment he emerged again with the small black case Curly had seen him open the Sunday before in church.

"Open it," ordered Spuds.

"It's locked."

"Well, unlock it."

Taking his time—*probably trying to think of some way to get out of this*, Curly thought as the horse lurched again—James Walk fished in his pocket until he came up with a key that he slowly turned in the lock.

"Hurry up!" snapped Spuds. Then, when he saw the contents of the case, he said, "That'll do. Lock it up again and toss me the key."

Walk did as he was told.

"Now, put that case down by the side of the road, nice and easy like, then get back in the coach and get outta here."

The coach was rumbling on down the road almost before Curly realized it was all over. They'd done it! They'd robbed the coach! Jake and Shorty ran over to Spuds and demanded that he show them the money.

"Not here, you fools. We gotta get out o' here. There'll be plenty of time to gloat over our loot later." He picked up the case and headed off at a trot through the trees.

Curly scurried after the men, slipping and sliding on the icy places. He could hardly keep from laughing with glee. They'd done it! He was rich!

And then, as they ran along, he realized that the footprints of the men ahead of him were leaving a trail so clear that a blind person could follow it. And when he turned and looked behind him, his prints were just as clear in the thin layer of snow.

Chapter 4

Betrayal

BACK IN LONDON, the four bandits stumbled into the Cracker Box Inn shortly after noon. They were tired, cold, and wet, but they had a satchel full of money.

"Order whatever you want, boys," grinned Spuds. "It's time to celebrate."

"I'd rather you just give me my cut of the loot and let me get outta here," said Shorty behind his cupped hand.

"Don't worry! Don't worry! You'll get your share, but we can't go passing money around in here," protested Spuds. "Someone would see us and ask questions."

"Well, then, how are you going to pay for a celebration without opening that case and showing it off to anyone who's looking?" Jake asked.

A sly grin spread over Spuds' red face as he pulled Mr. Walk's wallet from his pocket. "I think there's enough in here to pay for all we can eat or drink. So eat up; it's on me."

"What's on you?" Jake scowled. "That's common property. It came from the job. All for one and one for all. You can't claim that money!"

"Calm down. I was just funnin' you."

Curly had two big bowls of mutton and dumplings and a pint of ale. He finished with slices of sharp cheese and an apple. It was a feast, and his stomach was so full when they left the pub he thought he was going to burst. "This is livin'," he said to his comrades.

The three men had all had too much to drink and were talking loudly and slapping each other on the back with congratulations. "Come on," said Shorty, "let's split that money now."

"Yeah, give us our share," Jake demanded.

"What? Divide it up right here on the street? Maybe I should just throw it up in the air and let the wind blow away all the bills."

They were passing St. James's Park, and Spuds finally agreed to find a secluded place in the park where they could divide the spoils. When they had huddled under some bushes, Spuds first divided the money in half, and then divided one half to give Jake and Shorty each a quarter.

"Hey," said Shorty when he saw how the cut was going, "you better divide that three ways. You got no cause to keep half of it. We're all in this equal, remember?"

"Sure, I remember. That's why I'm cutting it four ways. The kid did his part, too."

"Yeah, so give me my cut," Curly ordered as firmly as he could muster.

"Wait a minute. Wait a *minute*," challenged Jake. "You never said this kid got a cut. He just came along with you. He's your responsibility." As he talked, Jake got red-faced and finally made a grab for the money.

Spuds whipped out his gun and commanded, "Back off, Jake. Four's in this thing, so we each get one fourth. No more. Now, take it or leave it."

Watching Spuds out of the corner of his eye, Jake reached out and carefully picked up his share and began stuffing the bills and coins into his pockets. Shorty did the same.

"You boys be careful with that, too. Don't go flashing it around. Look out there, Shorty, some of those bills are fallin' out of your pocket. If you guys turn up rich, spending money wherever you go, somebody's gonna get suspicious. Don't forget, that money came from right here in London, so the police are gonna be asking questions."

"Don't you worry about us," snarled Shorty as he and Jake got up and backed away.

"Now, how about my share?" said Curly when the two men had left.

"Here you go," said Spuds, holding out a meager handful of small coins toward the boy. "Don't spend it all at once," he laughed.

"Wait a minute!" barked Curly, refusing to take it. "That's not my full share. I get a full quarter. You just told them so."

"Of course, you do. But you don't have any place to keep it, so I'll keep it for you. Come on and take this; then whenever you need more, I'll give you some."

"No, no. I want my full share now. I can figure how to take care of it. But first I want my share."

"Calm down, kid," said Spuds as he put the money back into the case and closed it up. "You don't need all this money at one time. It's safer if I keep it for you."

"I want my money—now!"

"Well, I ain't giving it to you, and that's final. You'd just attract attention with it, and then the police would be on us in no time. Come on. Let's get back to the warehouse. I'm tired and need some sleep." Spuds got up and began walking out of the park.

Curly went running after him, cursing and yelling, "You thief! Give me my share!" But Spuds walked on, looking straight ahead, as if Curly were of no more concern to him than a mosquito. Out of desperation and anger, Curly grabbed the back of Spuds' coat and pulled with all his might. "Give me my money!"

Spuds swung around and hit Curly across the head with a vicious backhand swing. It knocked the boy to the ground, but that made him all the more angry. He jumped to his feet and charged at the man. "Give me my money or I'll . . . I'll—"

His mind scrambled for a

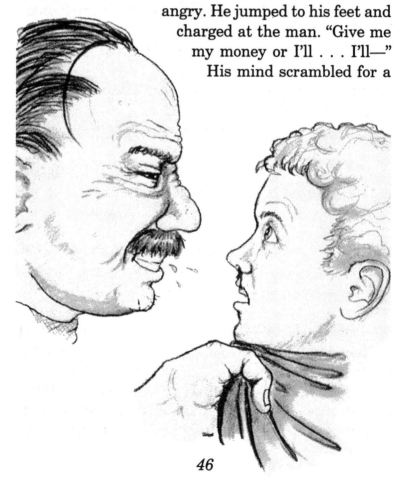

threat. "Or I'll go tell the church people that you were the bandit!"

Spud's homely face screwed up into a red knot, and he lunged at Curly, grabbing the boy with his free hand. Then he dropped the case and began beating the youngster. Curly tried to ward off the blows with his upraised arms, but he also looked for the opportunity to break free, grab the satchel of money, and run. *This could be my chance*, he thought wildly, but the blows fell harder and harder until Curly's only hope was to break free and escape.

Finally, the blows stopped. "Don't you ever grab me, and don't you ever threaten me again, boy," Spuds snarled, still holding Curly's coat with one hand, "or I'll beat you within an inch of your life."

Just then Curly managed to twist free. His nose was bleeding, and tears were streaming down his face. It was all he could do to get away, and he made no attempt to grab the money as he ran back into the park.

He ran and ran until his legs were as wobbly as a wilted plant. Finally, he sank to the ground by a board fence in an alley in an unfamiliar part of town. He sat there, leaning his head against the fence, his breath coming in great gasps. He couldn't help himself. Loud sobs wrenched out from his gut, and he began to cry. Everything had gone wrong. He'd been betrayed, and now there was no place to turn.

Curly's head and arms were throbbing from Spuds' beating, but the pain inside was worse. His whole life had been one big betrayal—starting with his father. The man who should have loved him had turned on him, beat him, and drank up all the family's food money. He hated his father. "If he'd been a decent man, I wouldn't be living on the street," Curly moaned.

Some time later a cold rain roused the boy, and Curly got up painfully and began to search for someplace to get out of the weather. Behind a big stone wall surrounding the garden of a fancy house he found a dustbin full of old clothes and other trash. It had a wooden lid—probably intended to keep out the rats—but it gave him extra protection from the rain. Pulling the rags over him, Curly fell into a fitful sleep.

He dreamed about his mother. He could see her clearly, and even in his dream he thought this was unusual because it had been a long time since he could remember her face. It made him feel warm inside when he awoke, and he tried to keep her image in his mind, but within a few minutes it had slipped away and all he had left was a vague sense of her warm smile and soft embrace, surrounded by the angry yells of his drunken father.

He crawled out of the dustbin to find the morning well spent. He had gone to sleep before dark and slept all night and through the morning. But now he was hungry again. The rain had stopped, and so he went scrounging in the garbage cans behind the wealthy homes looking for something to eat. He found half a loaf of bread, but ate only the part that wasn't soggy. A few orange peels were the only other edible things he found.

When the pale winter sun was as high in the sky as it would get for that time of year, Curly decided to head back to the warehouse. *Maybe Spuds is sober now and has come to his senses enough to give me my share of the money.*

But as he walked through the streets of London toward the warehouse, a plan began to take shape in Curly's mind. If Spuds refused to give him his fair share of the money, he had a pretty good idea where Spuds would have hid it—in the space behind the loose stone in the wall. Curly decided that even if Spuds still refused to give him his share, he would act pleasantly so that he wouldn't raise the man's suspicions. Then he would look for an opportunity to take what was rightfully his.

Sooner or later, he figured, Spuds would be out of the warehouse long enough to make it safe for him to take the money. Then he would leave town. He began imagining where he would go. *I'd have enough money to go wherever I want*, he thought. Maybe he'd return to his hometown north of London and search for some of his sisters and brothers. But a cold fear dampened that idea: Spuds would probably search for him there as soon as he realized Curly had left London—he had never made a secret of his past.

Maybe I should go to France or America or maybe a South Sea island. The thought of all the exotic places he might travel to excited him, and he hurried along the street.

When he got to the warehouse, Spuds was busy

with a "customer," and said to Curly, "I see you're back. Get on out to the street and keep a watch for us. Run along now." No mention was made of the beating. It was like it hadn't happened.

Curly turned and went to the large front door of the warehouse where he could watch up and down the street while Spuds conducted his business. When the customer left, he returned and asked Spuds, "How come you're still trying to make these little deals when we got all that money from the holdup? I should think you'd retire in style." He had no sooner said the words than he realized he was lucky to have found Spuds. The old man might have packed up and fled the old warehouse just like Curly was planning to do.

"Why haven't I *retired?*" said Spuds with a wry grin. "For the same reason I didn't give you your full share of the money. I'm protecting our interests, of course."

"How d'you mean?"

"Many people in this city know me, including the police. If they start askin' around about anyone who has suddenly started livin' high off the hog, I wouldn't want my name to come up. You get my drift?"

"No."

"Look, after a heist like we pulled, the first thing the police watch for is someone flashin' a lot of new money. That person becomes a prime suspect. So, I want the word to get around that it's business as usual for me. That way, I won't be a suspect."

Curly nodded. "That's smart. But, now can I have

my money? I won't go flashin' it around."

"Here, I'll give you whatever you need today but no more. I'm not going to take the risk." Spuds held out his hand with two shillings in it. "You gotta understand, kid. People would get suspicious if an urchin like you started flashing five-pound notes around."

"But I wouldn't do that."

Spuds didn't flinch. He continued to hold out the money and looked steadily at Curly.

Finally, the boy took the coins and looked the other way to hide his frustration. At that moment he decided he was going to have to take matters into his own hands.

Chapter 5

The Raid

B Y SUNDAY, Curly had not yet found an opportunity to take his money from the hole in the wall. Spuds had been true to his word, giving the boy a few coins each day, but Curly knew that it would take years to get his fair share at that rate.

Curly left the warehouse. "He's treating me like his slave," he muttered to himself as he walked down the cobblestone street, scuffing his old shoes with every step. His hands were stuffed in his pockets, and he'd pulled his cap low over his eyes. *He makes me stay in that cold, filthy warehouse working for a few coins. At least if I was working at a regular job I could quit if I wanted to.*

"I gotta get my money and get out," he said aloud.

He looked up and realized that he'd wandered

onto Oxford Street from where he could see the steeple of St. George's Church a couple blocks away. Had it been only two weeks ago since he'd lowered himself from the steeple and almost fallen off the roof? Somehow it seemed more like a year.

Then Curly remembered the woman with the gray shawl and her little girl who looked so much like his sister. It occurred to him that if he left London, he wouldn't see her again, and it made him homesick. He no longer knew exactly what his sister looked like, and that little girl was the last reminder he had of her.

The memory gnawed at him as he walked along. *Maybe I could see her one more time*, he thought.

Then the bells of St. George's began to ring, and he realized the service was about to start. It helped him make up his mind. He waited until most of the people had entered the church, then he went in and found a seat in the back row. But try as he did, he could not find the woman in the gray shawl sitting in the rows in front of him.

He stretched his neck and began a second search of each row, trying to imagine what she would look like if she were wearing something other than the gray shawl. At one point he thought he had found her near the front on the far side, but when the woman turned and he caught a glimpse of the side of her face, she had such a big nose that he knew he was mistaken.

And then Curly remembered the balcony. *She must be up there*, he thought. When everyone stood for the reading of the Gospel, he slipped out and went searching for the stairs leading from the lobby to the balcony.

He was halfway up when someone came around the corner at the top and started down. Curly looked up and was horrified: It was Mr. Walk! It had never crossed his mind that he might run into the man if he showed his face around the church again.

His first urge was to run, but he feared that would attract too much attention. So he ducked his head and hoped that since Walk was coming down from above him, the man wouldn't notice his face if he kept his head down like he was looking where he was going.

Whether it worked, he wasn't sure, but the man did not say anything, and they passed each other without slowing their pace. Curly wanted to turn around but dared not. On up he went and entered the right side of the balcony. An usher smiled at him and pointed to a seat, but Curly continued walking all the way across the back of the balcony behind the rows and out the door on the other side.

Trying to avoid making any noise, he went down the other stairs. Once he regained the empty lobby, he ducked out the front door, ran down the steps, and kept running down the street. He vowed never to go near St. George's again and never to tell Spuds that he'd been there.

What Curly didn't realize was that Mr. Walk *had* seen him and thought the boy looked vaguely familiar. Later, sitting in the pew listening to the lengthy sermon, the man suddenly realized that he was the boy who had secured the horses when the coach had been robbed! Slipping out of the pew, the man ran upstairs and diligently searched the balcony.

The more Mr. Walk thought about the boy, the more certain he was that he had seen him at St. George's before. That would explain how the bandits knew about the money shipment and why the kid had yelled, "That's him!" when he had stepped down from the coach.

He discussed his suspicions with one of the members of the committee for Müller's Orphan Home, and the man said, "If you've seen him at least twice here in St. George's, he probably lives in the neighborhood."

"I doubt that the kid has any family," said Walk. "I noticed him because he looks so scruffy, and I've never seen him with anyone else . . . except out on the road. And I certainly hope none of those bandits was his father."

"Whether he has family nearby or not, I have no idea," said the other committee member, "but he's obviously fallen in with a bad crowd."

"Maybe I'll spend a little extra time wandering the streets," Walk mused. "Who knows, I might run into him again. We might get some of the orphan money back after all."

"Have you forgotten? It's the middle of winter!"

"No," Walk shrugged with a wry smile, "but some days it's not so bad out."

Three days later Curly was on his way back to the warehouse after buying a new pair of shoes when he had the distinct impression that someone was following him. He wasn't sure whether he had seen someone out of the corner of his eye or noticed a strange look on the faces of the people coming toward him on the sidewalk.

The hunch was so strong that he turned around several times to see if he could catch someone following him, but he had no luck. Finally, he gave up, telling himself his imagination was playing tricks on him.

His new shoes were for a purpose. He had convinced Spuds to let him get new clothes, and the shoes were the last of his shopping. He wanted to have clothes for traveling, because this was the night he planned to take his money and leave town.

Spuds always stayed out late Wednesday nights at the Cracker Box to gamble with some of his friends. Curly usually went along and did acrobatic tricks to earn a little change. Last week he had protested going because he had enough money already.

Earlier that day Spuds had said, "You'll be doing some tricks at the Cracker Box tonight like usual. Things can't appear too different with us, or we'll attract attention. You already look peculiar in all those new clothes."

"Then maybe I shouldn't be doing tricks!"

"You'll do tricks. There's gotta be some excuse for you having enough money for new clothes."

"Then I want enough money to buy new shoes," bargained Curly.

Spuds looked down at the boy's feet. "Well, I have to admit yours are falling off your feet. All right, get the new shoes, but don't wear them tonight."

Curly agreed.

His plan was to go to the pub with Spuds, do a few tricks, and then tell Spuds that he didn't feel well and was going back to the warehouse. Once there, he would take his share of the loot and head out on his own.

However, as he walked back toward the warehouse in the late afternoon, his new shoes pinched his feet, and he decided to try one more time to get Spuds to give him his money. *It'd be better if Spuds and I were on good terms and I didn't have to leave town*, he thought. Spuds was usually a decent guy—but he could be nasty to his enemies.

"Help me move these barrels," Spuds ordered when Curly came in. "A new shipment's coming in tomorrow, and I need to make space for it."

The two sweated and groaned as they wrestled the barrels into their new positions. When they took a break around the stove in the corner of the warehouse that Spuds called "home," Curly raised the subject of his money again. "Spuds, I've been learning a lot from how you've been handling our money. I can see how to do it myself, now. You know—not spending too much at one time, not making myself look rich all of a sudden. Don't you think I've learned enough to receive my full share now?"

Spuds looked at the boy for a long time without changing his expression, and hope grew in Curly's heart. But when he spoke, he said, "Don't try to flatter me by tellin' me what a good teacher I am. It won't do you no good. I'm not going to give you all that money at once. Besides, the fact that you're always asking for it shows me you haven't learned much."

"What do you mean? I've been learnin'."

"You only want it because you want to do something different with it than what I've been doing. Anything different's gonna attract attention."

"No," objected Curly, his voice rising. "I'm not gonna to spend it all at once, if that's what you're thinkin'."

Spuds face got red as he yelled, "Then why do you want it?"

"I want it 'cause it's mine!"

"Well, I ain't gonna give it to ya, so shut up!" bellowed Spuds.

Suddenly, the warehouse door burst open as though an explosion had gone off outside and five policemen came pouring into the warehouse. Spuds dove for his cot and pulled his pistol out from under his pillow where he had been keeping it—for "better protection," he'd said—since they'd come back from the robbery. He pointed the gun at first one policeman, then another.

None of the London police were armed, but they bravely stood their ground not giving Spuds or Curly a chance to make a break for the front or rear door. Finally, one of the policemen said, "Don't you think you better put that away, Baxter?"

"Put it away?" Spuds asked, incredulous. His eyes were wide, and he was breathing harder than when they had finished moving the

barrels. "I'm not puttin' it away until you get outta my way and give me a clear path from here."

The officer tipped his head to one side and said, "Don't be foolish, man. That pistol holds one shot. The most you could do is shoot one of us, and then the other four would be all over you, and you'd be up for murder if the man you shot died. Besides, we got men outside—both front and back."

Though no one had told him to, Curly slowly raised his hands. It seemed like the right thing to do, like the men on the coach had done when they had robbed it.

"You don't want to face murder now, do you, Spuds?" Apparently the officer in charge knew Spuds from some previous crime.

Spuds' arm ceased to swing back and forth pointing the pistol randomly at the policemen, and he slowly let it drop to his side.

"Now you're being smart, man," said the officer. "You just drop it there on your bed, and everything'll be fine."

Once Spuds had surrendered, the head officer called out the door, "You can come in now, sir."

Curly stared in disbelief as James Walk and another policeman came through the warehouse door. Walk looked first at Curly and then at Spuds. "Yes, sir," he said. "These are two of them—there's no mistake about it. The other two I never saw, but concerning these I'm prepared to swear in court. That one," he pointed to Spuds, "was the ringleader, doing all the talking and holding the gun on me.

60

That is a face I'll never forget."

"Then I guess it's time to go down to the station," said the officer. "A police wagon should have arrived by now. Put the shackles on 'em and let's be off. You other men—search this place, see if you can find the money."

One of the policemen came forward and put chains around each of Spuds' ankles. He then started to do the same to Curly when Mr. Walk spoke up. "Is it necessary for the boy?" he asked.

"It's a matter of policy, sir. These young 'uns can bolt like a scared rabbit. We can't take chances."

Curly had never experienced such a terrible feeling as when the policeman locked the rings around each of his ankles and he heard the chain clink to the floor between them. When they gave him a little push, he shuffled toward the door. This was it; his whole life was ended. *I'll be in prison until I die.*

Spuds followed him through the door and muttered when they were close together, "So, you think you've learned how to handle money without drawing attention to yourself, do you?"

Chapter 6

"His Kind Are No Good"

CURLY AND SPUDS SAT on opposites sides of the police wagon as it rattled along the street. It was dark inside with the only light coming through a small, bar-covered window in the back.

Curly wished Spuds would say something to him. He didn't like Spuds thinking he'd betrayed them. In his mind, he kept going over what he had done and with whom he had talked. He couldn't think of any time he had flashed money around—after all, Spuds had never given him more than what he needed.

Finally, he spoke up. "What makes you think it's my fault the police were onto us? You never gave me any extra money."

Spuds grunted but didn't answer.

That made Curly angry. He wasn't going to be

blamed for something he hadn't done. "Maybe it was you last Wednesday night at the Cracker Box," he accused. "Maybe someone at the pub was an informer. After all, you were buying drinks for everyone in the whole place, and that's not very common."

"That wasn't it," Spuds finally answered. "I been thinking, it might have been Shorty or Jake. Maybe they got picked up and snitched on us . . . though it's hard for me to think they'd do that to an old partner. I've known those buzzards for years.

"Look," Spuds continued, "no matter what they say or do at the police station, don't say nothing about the money. Don't say how much we have or anything. Understand?"

"Sure," agreed Curly, as the wagon came to a stop. He was eager to gain Spuds' confidence again. "How would I know about the money? You didn't give me any more than a few coins at a time."

"That's right, and now you know why. The police can't pressure you to turn it over to them, 'cause you've never had your hands on it. See? I wasn't so dumb."

The door in the back of the wagon opened, and a policeman started giving orders. "Come on, boys. Head on into the station. Watch your step, now."

It was hard walking with the chains on their ankles, and once they were in a cell, Spuds asked the jailer, "Can't you take these shackles off? There's no way we're gonna make a break for it now that we're behind bars."

"You'll have to speak to Officer Bradley," said the

jailer. "He put them on, not me."

A few minutes later, the officer named Bradley came into their cell, unlocked their ankle chains, then sat down on a bench. "Well, Spuds, looks like you did it this time. I didn't think you'd stoop to something like this—stealing money from church people. You're going to pay for this one a long time."

Spuds shrugged, but the mention of the church reminded Curly that he'd almost run into James Walk at St. George's the previous Sunday. Suddenly, his heart sank. Had Walk recognized him after all when they met on the stairs and set about trying to track him down? He also recalled his impression that someone was following him earlier that day. *Maybe* . . . Curly thought as he glanced guiltily at Spuds. *Maybe I was the one who led the police to the warehouse after all!*

The next morning Curly and Spuds were awakened by the arrival of their unhappy partners in crime, Jake and Shorty. How the police tracked them down, Curly was unable to discover. After a breakfast of mush and tea, Officer Bradley came to their cell, took Jake out, then relocked the door.

"What's going on?" asked Curly, watching Jake shuffle down the hall.

"They're going to interrogate us," said Spuds gloomily.

"What's that?" It sounded terrible, like torture.

"It means they're going to question us about the robbery, so remember what I told you about the money. And if you double-cross us, boy, we'll find a way to hurt you bad."

Each of the men was taken out of the cell and brought back a half hour later. Curly was the last to be called. "Don't forget," hissed Spuds as they passed each other at the door of the cell.

In the small office where Officer Bradley took him, there was another policeman standing by the door—and sitting in a straight wooden chair was James Walk.

"Sit down," Bradley ordered, pointing to a chair in the middle of the room. Then he walked around an old desk and took a seat on the other side. He leaned back in the chair and clasped his hands together across his ample stomach, interlacing his fingers. "Well, son, what do you have to say for yourself?"

"Nothin'," mumbled Curly.

"Speak up. We're not going to hurt you."

"I said, nothin'."

"Where's your family, young man?" asked James Walk from the side.

"Don't got any."

"Listen, boy. It'll go better for you if you cooperate with us." Officer Bradley leaned forward and stabbed a finger in Curly's direction. "You can't gain anything by being stubborn."

"I'm not being stubborn," said Curly, his eyes flashing. "My old man died six years ago—my ma, too. Don't know where any of my brothers and sisters are; we got split up."

"Is this Spuds character some relative of yours?" asked Walk.

"No. He just lets me stay with him."

"Tell us about the money you took," said Bradley impatiently. The officer didn't care about the kid's family; he had a crime to solve.

"Uh—I never got any," said Curly, biting his lip and trying to remember how Spuds had told him to answer.

"Oh?" said the officer, arching an eyebrow. "We recovered part of the money from the other two bandits, and they said Spuds divided the money four ways—one quarter for each of you. Where's your share?"

"Spuds kept it. He only gave me a little at a time," said Curly truthfully, but his mind was racing. The officer said they'd recovered some of the money from the other two . . . did that mean they hadn't found the money in the warehouse?

"Why'd he do that?" The officer was still speaking to him.

"Uh—what?"

"Your share—why didn't Spuds give it to you?"

"He was afraid I'd flash it around and get us caught."

"Hmm." Officer Bradley's eyes narrowed. "Did you see where he stashed it?"

"No." That was the truth; Curly hadn't actually *seen* where Spuds put the money, though he was pretty sure it was in the secret place behind the loose stone in the wall. "Whenever he gave me any money, he just took it from his pocket."

"Sounds like Spuds," muttered Bradley. "He's a sly fox—probably planned to keep it all for himself." The officer jerked his thumb toward the door. "Guess we're done with you, boy. You can go on back to the cell." And he motioned for the policeman standing by the door to escort Curly back down the hall.

"Hold on a minute, Officer," James Walk interrupted. "What about the plan I suggested to you about the boy?"

"Oh. Right. Well, I suppose so," said Bradley, "but I think you're wasting your time . . . and taking a big risk. I tell you, his kind are no good. He'll be in trouble again before you can turn around."

"Thank you for your advice, sir. I'm sure there's a high possibility you are correct. But we must try for a change; without my plan, I see no hope for the boy."

"Well, do as you please," said Bradley. "Stop at the desk to sign the custody papers."

"Come on, son," Walk said to Curly. "You can come with me."

Curly was startled. "Where are we going?"

"Out of jail. Isn't that good enough for you for now?"

Confused, Curly followed the man down the hall—the opposite direction from the jail cells. At the front desk, Mr. Walk busied himself for several minutes talking to the desk sergeant and signing some papers. Then at the front door of the station, Mr. Walk turned to Curly and said, "I'm not going to put any shackles on you, but I need to warn you: The police have released you into my custody. If you run away, they'll bring you back and put you in jail for good, and I won't be around to get you out. Do you understand?"

Curly nodded, not knowing exactly what he was agreeing to, except that he wasn't supposed to run away.

Outside, Curly was surprised to see the same black coach Mr. Walk had been traveling in when they had robbed him on the road to Bristol. There was the same driver and coachman who opened the door for both of them.

As they took their seats in the coach—Mr. Walk sitting in the back seat facing forward and Curly sitting across from him facing backward—Curly noticed the man lift a small case onto his lap and hold it tightly.

Noticing Curly's curiosity about the case, Walk said, "Yes, this is the money we recovered from those other two scoundrels, but I warn you. The coachman is armed, and if you try anything on this trip, he is authorized to shoot."

The coach lurched away from the curb and with a swinging motion headed down the street behind the clip-clopping horses. "Where are we going?" asked Curly.

"You ought to be able to figure that one out for yourself," the man said, looking out the window at the passing buildings.

Chapter 7

Ashley Downs

THEY HAD BEEN TRAVELING on the road toward Bristol
for about an hour, when suddenly the countryside began to look familiar to Curly. The fields had
given way to sparse woods. Then the coach splashed
through a puddle at the bottom of a draw and started
up a small hill.

"Do you recognize where we are?" asked James
Walk.

Curly glanced at him, then looked back out the
window. The area appeared different without the
snow and ice, but there was no question. "Yeah," he
muttered sheepishly. "I guess this is where we
stopped your coach a couple weeks back."

"Where you *robbed* me is more like it. Did you
ever think about the possibility that someone could

have gotten killed that day?"

"Spuds didn't want no bloodshed," Curly said defensively.

"Oh, he didn't, did he? Well, I'm glad to hear it, but things can go wrong, you know. What would have happened if the coachman had drawn his gun? One of the other bandits would have shot him, and Spuds might have shot me. Several people could have died."

"Jake and Shorty didn't have no guns," said Curly with a smile. Their little trick had fooled 'em, all right.

"What?"

"I said they didn't have any guns. Only Spuds had a gun—his pistol. The other two were supposed to pretend they had guns but stay out of sight behind the coachman's back so he wouldn't know the difference."

"You mean to say we were robbed by a gang with only one pistol? That's incredible." James Walk shook his head, and his face had a funny look, like he was going to laugh. . . or cry. "Still, someone could have gotten shot," he said finally. "It was a terrible thing you did. Do you realize that?"

Curly just looked out the window. He'd never really thought of it like that. All he'd wanted was some money. After all, nobody had ever done anything for him his whole life. Why not take something for himself?

That evening they stopped in the town of Reading, and Mr. Walk got two rooms in an inn overlooking the Thames River. After a fine supper, the driver and the coachman went to the room they shared, and Mr. Walk took Curly to their room. But before he blew out the lamp, Mr. Walk locked the door and pinned the key inside a pocket in his sleeping shirt.

A strange feeling came over Curly. For the first time since leaving London, it struck him that he wasn't really free. Yes, he knew Mr. Walk had insisted on his coming with him, and he wasn't supposed to run away or he'd get put back in jail, but . . . locking the door—that was still like keeping him a prisoner.

I'm pretty good at picking pockets, thought Curly. *I could get that key away from him easy, especially when he falls asleep.* As he lay in bed in the dark, he considered taking the key and escaping. But where would he go once he got outside the inn? If he went back to the warehouse, the police would pick him up in no time. And that dinner Mr. Walk paid for was a pretty good feed. Maybe he ought to see what the man was up to. They were going to Bristol to deliver what was left of the money—that much he had figured out. He'd wait and see what happened next. There'd be time to escape later if he needed to.

They arose early and were on the road as the sun came up. "We have farther to go today than we did yesterday if we want to get to Ashley Downs by nightfall," said Mr. Walk.

"Get where?" asked Curly. He thought they were going to Bristol.

"Ashley Downs—near Bristol, of course."

"Why?"

"Haven't you figured that out yet? If I can't deliver all the money our church raised to help George Müller in his mission, I thought I'd bring him a helper."

Curly let the subject drop and looked out the window to watch the farms and villages they were driving through. What did Mr. Walk mean? Was he going to stay and help that Mr. . . . whatever his name was? If so, what was he going to do with Curly? He wouldn't just dump him, would he—way out here in the middle of nowhere? It would take him a couple of weeks to walk back to London—and there was a lot of countryside between villages. It'd be hard to beg food on the way. And where would he sleep? It was winter . . . Curly shook the worrisome thoughts away, sank down on the swaying seat, and slept.

The coach rolled into Bristol before dark but did not stop. Curly began again to worry about what was going to happen when they got there. Would Mr. Walk tell the orphan man that he was the thief that had stolen their money? Was he going to get a beating? Sensing Curly's nervousness, James Walk announced, "Only a little farther now to Ashley Downs."

"What's Ashley Downs—a village?" asked Curly.

"Not exactly," Mr. Walk laughed. "Ashley Downs is the name of George Müller's orphan home. And . . . looks like we've arrived."

Curly peered out the window guiltily as the coach stopped before a large gate. An attendant opened the gate, and the coach made its way up a drive toward some large buildings at the top of a hill. Dozens of kids were running around, all dressed warmly in caps and coats and shoes. Some were playing games; some were obviously working. The gate closed, and Curly flopped back in his seat. He didn't want to get out and get stared at by those other kids. Did they all know he was the bandit that had stolen their money?

But James Walk motioned him to get out first, so Curly climbed out of the coach and stood by the large wheel while Mr. Walk got out. "Quite some place, isn't it?" the man said, surveying the large brick dormitories and brown fields surrounded by stone walls. Curly looked too but did not respond. "Stay right here," Walk ordered and knocked on the door of the nearest building.

Mr. Walk disappeared inside for sometime, and when he finally came out he was followed by an older man in a black suit. The older man stared intently at Curly as he walked across the yard toward the coach. He was straight and wiry with white hair and lambchop sideburns that covered his thin cheeks. The features of his face were sharp, giving him a stern appearance.

But when he stood directly in front of Curly, the stern face cracked into a smile. "So, this must be our young bandit."

Curly's heart sank. So, Mr. Walk *did* tell on him.

"Indeed, he is," responded James Walk. "Curly Roddy, this is Mr. George Müller, the director of this fine home."

Mr. Müller held out his hand. Curly was confused. No one had ever shaken hands with him before. But he took the man's big hand in his and managed to stammer, "Pleased to meet you, sir."

Mr. Müller then turned to James Walk and said, "Please extend our thanks to the members of St. George's Church for their kind generosity, and thank you, too, for bringing us the young Roddy boy.

I'm sure we'll get along fine. Are you sure you can't stay the night and leave in the morning?"

Curly's eyes widened and his mouth went dry. What? Mr. Walk was going to *leave* him at the orphan home?

"No, no," Mr. Walk was saying. "I have some other business to attend to in Bristol. Besides," and Mr. Walk jerked his head in Curly's direction, "it may be best to just get on with it as far as the lad goes."

Curly was suddenly in a panic. He was being put in an orphanage! That was almost as bad as prison. But before he could do or say anything, the two men shook hands, Mr. Walk climbed back into the coach, and drove away. Curly watched, stunned, as the big gates at the end of the drive closed behind the coach.

The full impact of the words, "If I can't deliver all the money . . . I thought I'd bring him as a helper," hit home. *He brought me here to be their slave*, thought Curly.

"Well, lad, if you'll come with me, I'll take you to your bed." Mr. Müller's voice broke into Curly's shocked thoughts. "Tomorrow in the daylight someone will show you all around Ashley Downs." Not knowing what else to do at the moment, Curly followed Mr. Müller, who led the way up the stairs at a fast pace, not at all in keeping with his age. They entered a large room the full width of the whole building. Several windows lined each side, through which Curly could see the fading pink in the night's purple sky.

Mr. Müller stopped to light a lamp and then continued down the center of the room between the two rows of narrow beds. "Your bed is number twenty-two," he announced. "Right here." The man pointed a bony finger at a bed with two blankets folded at the foot. "It's not fancy, but you'll find it a mite more comfortable than a jail cell. I know . . ." He paused for emphasis and turned to look at Curly.

The boy caught his meaning. "You mean you . . .?" he ventured as a bell outside the dormitory began to ring.

"That's right, lad." He smiled. "I was only a little older than you when I spent my first night in prison. And you can be sure I didn't get away with only one night behind bars like you did. I was in there nearly a month for my sinful ways. I'll tell you about it sometime. But right now, it's time to eat. That bell was the supper bell."

Curly could hardly imagine that Mr. Müller had ever been a kid like himself—much less in prison. But he didn't have time to think about it as he followed the older man down to a large, noisy dining room with three rows of tables with benches on each side. Behind the benches stood at least a hundred boys and about a dozen men. Each boy was dressed in a uniform of brown corduroy trousers and navy-blue jacket buttoned up to a white starched collar. Curly thought the uniform looked very uncomfortable, but when he glanced down at his own clothes he felt very out of place, even though he had on the new clothes he'd bought with the robbery money.

"Boys," Mr. Müller announced in a booming voice that silenced the noise and voices in the dining hall, "we have a new boy. Please meet Master Curly Roddy."

"Welcome, Master Roddy," everyone chorused together. Whispering began immediately, and Curly knew they were talking about him.

"You can sit right there," Mr. Müller said quietly to Curly, pointing to an empty place at the end of a bench. Then he raised his hand and his loud voice again. "Let's pray. Dear Father, we thank You for what You have given us to eat this evening, and thank You for the new lad you have brought to our home. Amen."

The boys climbed over the benches and took their seats—all except one boy near the center of each table who remained standing. From a pot before him, he spooned a thick soup into bowls and handed them to a boy on each side of him who passed them along. Next came a platter of bread, and the boys began to eat.

No one spoke directly to Curly, but the boys near him kept whispering to each other. For the first time that Curly could remember, he was not hungry when food was in front of him. He played with his soup and took small bites of bread that would barely go down when he tried to swallow.

After supper, the boys began to file out of the dining room. "You're on cleanup," announced the biggest boy from Curly's table, pointing directly at him.

Curly just stood there, not knowing what to do until one of the men called to the big boy and said, "Roger, I think you're on cleanup tonight. Go back and take care of your table."

The boy sneered at Curly as he came back to the table. Curly returned the glare and left with the rest of the boys. As the group pushed through the doorway into the dormitory, he heard somebody behind him snicker, "He's got fancy new clothes, but looks like he hasn't had a bath in a year."

That was enough. Curly didn't ask to be here, and he didn't have to put up with being heckled by a bunch of pampered country boys. In a flash he whirled around and grabbed the first kid behind him. "Who you talking about?" he demanded. It made no difference to Curly whether he had the right boy or not. Holding him by the front of his jacket, he pushed him backward until he slammed into the wall, knocking the breath out of the surprised boy. "I'll teach you not to fool with me," Curly said. Sticking his foot out, he pulled the boy forward so that he fell flat on his face on the floor.

Everyone else had backed off, making a circle around the boys. Curly was about to jump on his downed victim, when someone grabbed his shoulder from behind and spun him around. It was Roger, the boy who was supposed to be downstairs cleaning up the table.

Roger pulled back his fist, ready to let Curly have it, but he was not prepared for a boy trained on the streets of London. Curly dropped down and plowed

right into Roger, tackling him around the middle and driving him back into the onlookers.

Both boys lost their balance and fell to the floor beside the first bed in the dormitory. The circle of observers regrouped around the new center of action as Roger and Curly rolled on the floor. For a moment Curly was on top, but somehow Roger bucked him off and spun around to grab him from behind. Unruffled, Curly grabbed the bigger boy's arm and flipped him across his hip and shoulder so that he landed on the floor in front of him.

Curly leaped on Roger again and rolled him onto his stomach. He positioned himself astride Roger's back, grabbed one of the boy's flailing arms, and pulled it around until he had it in a hammerlock. He was just beginning to apply enough pressure to make the bigger boy moan with pain when a man's stern voice boomed behind them. "That will be enough! Get up, both of you."

Chapter 8

The Leader of the Gang

THE MAN WHO HAULED THE BOYS off the floor was the headmaster for the boys' orphan house. He ordered Roger back downstairs to finish his kitchen duty and sent Curly to his bed.

That night, after the lamps were out, Curly lay on his cot thinking about London. His little corner in the warehouse with Spuds had been cold and dirty, and Spuds had even hit him sometimes, but life there was familiar. Curly longed to be back on the streets, free to run where he pleased. These kids all thought they were so smart, but he was sure they would never survive on the streets of London.

What Curly didn't know was that, like him, many of the boys had come from London or other cities like Bristol and Birmingham, as well as from small towns and the countryside. England had very few orphan houses, and those were reserved for children of the wealthy. Poor children who were orphaned were often left to beg and die on the streets or forced into workhouses where many died from the hard labor, twelve- to fourteen-hour workdays, poor food, and unsanitary conditions.

George Müller had started his orphan houses to help England's poor children—kids just like Curly. So Curly was by no means the only one of his kind at Ashley Downs. But that first night, he felt more alone than if he had been sleeping in a trash bin in an alley of the great city.

Early the next morning, the headmaster roused Curly out of bed and marched him off to measure him for clothes—uniforms like the other boys wore. Curly felt strange. The three suits of clothes he was given weren't new—probably outgrown by other orphan boys—but they were clean, neat, and well-mended. Even though Spuds had given him money to buy new clothes, he had never had an extra set.

"But first, you must bathe," ordered the master, and he marched Curly to a back room where a steaming tub of water stood. "If you don't do a good job yourself," warned the man, "Mrs. Bentley will be in to scrub your hide with a brush until it's as pink as a spring

rose—so do it right the first time."

Terrified by the idea of a strange woman giving him a bath, Curly scrubbed himself cleaner than he had ever been in his life, then dressed in the clothes he had worn to Ashley Downs. Just as he finished putting on his shoes, a heavyset woman came into the bathroom. "You'll have to take those city clothes off and put on a school uniform," she announced.

"But they're mine, and they're new," Curly protested.

"All right. I'll box them up and keep them for you. But you won't be needing them around here. At Ashley Downs everyone wears a school uniform. Now hurry up and change or you'll be late for breakfast. Though I can't imagine what we'll eat today," she murmured as she left with his clothes. "Last night there wasn't a thing in the kitchen."

Curly changed into one of the uniforms and looked down at the brown cords and blue jacket. He felt awkward. His stomach felt tight and he went cold all over. But he bravely left for the dining room and stood behind the bench at the same table where he had sat the night before. Everyone waited until Mr. Müller prayed, before sitting.

"What do you think we'll eat today?" said the boy next to him.

Curly shrugged, but the boy across the table said, "Yesterday we had bread and the day before hot applesauce. I'll bet it's bread again."

But in a moment, the boys assigned to serve each table came out of the kitchen with pots of mush that they spooned into bowls. Tea was poured, and Curly ate heartily.

"Hey, you look like one of us, now," said the boy across the table. "Where you from?"

"London," said Curly.

"Chester's from London," the boy said.

Curly made a face as though he was bored and a little annoyed. "Who's Chester?"

"He's that boy you were fighting last night before you beat up Roger."

Curly vaguely remembered the boy he had first grabbed, but more interesting was the speaker's conclusion that he had "beat up" Roger. He might've been getting the best of the bigger boy, but the schoolmaster had broken up the fight before he'd had a chance to really prove himself.

"Yeah, I remember him," said Curly. "From London, is he? Where're you from?"

"I's from Bristol. Me an' my little brother an' sister are all here at Ashley Downs."

A fleeting thought crossed Curly's mind: *I wish my kid sister was here.* But he quickly dismissed it. After all, he didn't even want to be here himself. But somewhere—deep down—he wished his sister could be at Ashley Downs . . . safe.

School was a new challenge to Curly. He had never been in a classroom before, and sitting all day trying to learn to read and write was hard. Many of the children who came to Ashley Downs had never been to school either, but Curly didn't know that, and at first he felt very stupid.

Numbers were a different matter, however. Living on the street he had learned to add and subtract on his own, so he fit right in with most of the kids his age who were just beginning to learn their multiplication tables.

Within a few days, Curly was amazing the other boys in his dorm with acrobatic tricks, and many begged him to teach them how to do flips or walk on their hands. By spring he had set up classes after school and charged for his instruction. In payment he collected money, stamps, and favors. It gave him status with the other boys. Roger remained hostile, but at least the bigger boy kept his distance and did nothing to start another fight with the popular new boy.

At night, when all was dark in the dormitory, Curly often dreamed of escaping from Ashley Downs. He decided that when he had collected enough money and stashed enough food, he would sneak out and return to London. Then one night an even bigger idea came to him. *I'm sure Spuds never told the police where he hid the money,* Curly thought. *But he's stuck in prison, and that money's just sittin' there. So I could go back to the warehouse and get it for myself.*

From then on, Curly's weeks were filled with planning. Even during school, he daydreamed about getting out the gate, catching a ride to London, sneaking into the warehouse, pulling out the loose stone where the money was surely hidden, and living like a king for the rest of his life.

Then Curly had another idea. He could collect some extra food for his trip and also gain status with the boys if he organized a gang to raid the kitchen at night—sort of a test of who was brave enough to pull such a stunt. When they heard Curly's idea, John, the boy who sat across from him at the table, and Chester joined in.

"We'll wait until everyone is asleep tonight," said Curly, "then sneak down and raid the kitchen."

"Why not the schoolmasters' kitchen?" Chester suggested. He had long ago forgiven Curly for slamming him up against the wall that first day, and enjoyed his status as "a London boy" along with Curly. "They must have some fine treats in there."

That night, Curly fell asleep waiting in the dark, and it was John who finally woke him with a gentle shake of his shoulder. "Don't you think everyone's asleep by now?" John whispered.

"What time is it?" asked Curly.

"I heard the big clock downstairs strike twelve."

"Oughtta be good enough," Curly whispered. "Where's Chester?"

"Still in bed."

The two boys shook Chester awake, then quietly made their way out of the dorm room, taking care not to trip over anyone's boots or a book that might have been left in the middle of the floor.

At the bottom of the stairs, they turned and crept down the dark hall. Suddenly, a door opened and a

shaft of light appeared on the floor, widened, and then Mrs. Bentley came out dressed in her housecoat and sleeping bonnet.

The boys flattened themselves against the wall and hoped fervently that she would go the other way. Instead, the round housekeeper turned toward them, but the door swung closed on its hinges and the hall was plunged once again in darkness. Mrs. Bentley shuffled forward, softly humming a tune to herself.

Curly had a hand on both boys. John was still as a mouse, but he could feel Chester's courage draining away as the younger boy tried to inch away. Curly grabbed tightly to his arm and pinned him to the wall. Their only chance was to remain completely still and hope that Mrs. Bentley passed them in the dark. If Chester made a break for it, the woman would hear them for sure.

Then, in a moment, she had swished past and turned the corner toward the washroom.

Quickly, the boys headed toward the masters' kitchen in the opposite direction. "Oh, no," whispered John, who arrived first. "It's locked."

"What'd you expect?" said Curly. "That's why I brought this." He pulled a table knife from his pocket, but it was too dark for anyone to see it.

"Brought what?" Chester whispered.

"My burglar tools," said Curly importantly and went to work on the door. There was a grating sound and then a click. The handle turned, and the door opened.

After the blackness of the hallway, the room was dimly lit in an eerie blue from the moonbeams streaming through the window. Once they closed the door, the boys began to explore the shelves. But all they found was one small bag of oats and a few apples.

"We better not take the apples," warned John as Curly passed them out. "They'd miss them for sure and know someone was in here."

"I don't care," said Curly bravely. But the other boys refused.

The young raiders searched high and low, but the kitchen was otherwise bare.

Just outside their dorm room, the three boys whispered an agreement to try the main kitchen the next night. "There's got to be food there," said Curly before the boys parted.

But the next night, standing successfully in the middle of the large boys' kitchen, the three boys again found nothing. "Where can it be?" said Curly in frustration. "They're hiding the food, that's what. We've got to find where they stashed it."

After a few moments, John said thoughtfully, "Mr. Müller often tells us that God gives us food each day . . . like in the Lord's Prayer: 'Give us this day our daily bread.' I never thought he meant it literally, but maybe—"

"That's crazy," Curly broke in. "The Lord's Prayer doesn't mean one day at time." *That's no better than livin' on the streets,* he thought. "There's got to be a full pantry around here somewhere—you know, barrels of corned beef, sacks of flour, big bins of carrots and potatoes."

"I dunno," said Chester. "I've never seen a full storeroom. Whenever I'm on kitchen duty and have to peel potatoes, I peel them all, and we eat them all that day."

"This doesn't make any sense," said Curly in disgust. "Let's get outta here."

Chapter 9

Caught Red-Handed

CURLY DECIDED he wouldn't lead his gang on another raid until he discovered exactly where the food was. If word got out that he couldn't even find food, it would make him look like a fool.

All that summer he explored Ashley Downs whenever he had the chance. When he was in one of the other orphan houses doing a chore, he would open every door he could when no one was looking. On several nights he made expeditions by himself to explore the various kitchens—the one in the infants' house, the various boys' houses, and even the girls' houses. He knew if he was caught there at night, he would be severely punished, but he pressed on trying to find where the food was kept. But his results were always the same: What food he found was no more than for the next day, maybe two, and would certainly be missed.

Then one night in September while he was exploring, he found himself outside George Müller's personal quarters. He tried the door handle; it wasn't locked. Turning it noiselessly, Curly slipped inside. Of course, there was no kitchen in the old man's apartment—he always ate in one of the children's houses—but Curly might find out something. *In fact*, he thought suddenly, *maybe the old man kept all the food hidden here!*

Curly stood in what looked like a sitting room as his eyes adjusted to the dim light. Then, through an open door into a bedroom, he saw Müller kneeling on the floor beside his bed . . . praying aloud. The room was small and furnished with only a small table and a straight-backed rocker besides a plain cot. A candle flickered on the little table beside the bed. Curly had started to back away from the open doorway when he realized that Müller, whose back was toward him, was praying for food.

"Oh, Lord," Müller was pleading in an earnest voice, "You know that we are out of money, and there is no food for tomorrow."

Suddenly the prayer stopped and, without turning around, Müller said, "Come on in here, young man. You can help me pray."

Curly was terrified at being caught by George Müller. If he dashed out the door right that minute, maybe the old man wouldn't know who he was. He knew he could outrun the old man in a flash, and he wanted to leave Ashley Downs, so why not tonight? But somehow his feet were planted to the floor.

Mr. Müller turned. "Come on, Curly. Don't just stand there." Curly found himself advancing timidly into the small room wondering how Müller had remembered his name among the hundreds of children at the orphanage. "Do you kneel when you pray?" the old man asked, looking up at the boy.

Curly shrugged.

"I don't like it much, either," said Müller. "I'll admit that it helps me concentrate, but my old knees can't take it for long. So what is best—pray longer or pray better? Only God knows, I suppose. Here," he said pointing to the end of his bed, "you sit there, and I'll use the rocker."

Curly sat stiffly on the edge of the bed ready to bolt out the still-open door. But the old man slowly rocked, his hands hooked over the arms of the wooden chair. "You've been here almost a year, am I right?"

Curly nooded his head slightly.

"Do you remember what I promised to tell you when you first came?" he finally asked.

Curly thought for a moment. Mr. Müller had made some curious comment about being in prison, but he didn't want to bring it up again if he had misunderstood. It might sound like he was accusing the old man of being a criminal, so he simply said, "We were talking about the night I spent in jail."

"That's right, and I told you that I was only a little older than you when I spent my first night in prison. But I didn't get away with only one night. I was quite a rascal in those days." He sat there rocking and watching Curly in the flickering candlelight.

Curly wanted to ask more, but, still scared about being caught, he just waited.

Finally, Mr. Müller said, "I was living near Wolfenbüttel's Castle when the police pulled me in. I was only sixteen, but I'd been living in style—far beyond what I could afford. I had run up such a debt that the innkeeper had me arrested. Of course, I didn't have a penny. I was supposed to be going to school to become a minister, but I had spent all my money playing cards and drinking. So, when I couldn't pay, they threw me in prison."

The old man rocked silently for several more minutes. "What happened then?" Curly finally dared to venture.

"Oh, my. I sat there in that damp, dark place for a couple of weeks—the food was terrible. Finally, I began thinking about my life and how rotten I'd been. I had stolen money from my own father—and two years earlier I had been so interested in partying that for several days my father couldn't even find me to tell me my mother was seriously ill. I played cards and drank until two o'clock Sunday morning, then staggered back to my room only to meet my sad father who told me that Mother had died in the night."

Curly's eyes widened in horror.

"At the time," Müller went on, "even that didn't slow me down. During the next two years, I studied occasionally but spent most of my time playing around, reading novels, drinking in taverns, and making weak resolutions to improve. But I'd break those promises as soon as I made them and ended up behaving even worse.

"I only began to think about my life after I'd sat in jail a couple of weeks. There's nothing like four blank walls and a locked door to make you think about what matters in life."

"How—how did you get out?" Curly asked.

"Oh, I can still remember that very well. It was January 12, 1822, when the guard unbolted my door and said, 'You're wanted at the police office. Follow me, please.' When I got there, the police officer said my father had sent the money to pay all my debts and my fine and that I was therefore free to leave."

"You must have had a very kind father," Curly said quietly.

"Yes and no," said Müller. "He bailed me out, but he never forgave me. I knew he despised me, which made me hate myself, and because I hated myself, I continued behaving just as badly, even worse. I began stealing from my friends. That is the difference with God."

"Of course!" said Curly. "God would never steal from His friends."

"No, no, of course not." The old man smiled. "But that's not what I meant. I meant that when *God* rescues us, He also forgives us, and that enables us to change, to start over." He rocked back and forth and then added, "Of course, we must accept His forgiveness and invite Christ His Son to live in our hearts.

"But enough preaching," Müller said abruptly. "You are here to help me pray, so let's get to it."

The old man hunched forward, clasped his hands, and once again began praying for God to provide the orphanage with food for the next day. After a few minutes of intense prayer, he suddenly stopped. Curly feared that the old man expected him to pray, too, so he kept his eyes tightly shut until Mr. Müller said, "Do you know why I established these orphan houses?"

"Wh—what?" stammered Curly when he realized Müller was speaking to him.

"I said, do you know why I built these orphan houses?"

Curly thought for a moment. The answer seemed obvious: "For the children . . . to give them a place to live."

"Ah, yes. That's part of it. Psalm sixty-eight, verse five, describes God as 'A Father to the fatherless.' Therefore, since He has promised to provide for the orphans, He can't fail."

All Curly could remember about his own father was the man drinking up their food money and beating them. Trusting in the goodness of a father didn't seem reasonable to him.

George Müller continued, "Thirty-six years ago I began taking in homeless children. And since then, through prayer, God has fed thousands and thousands of children just like you. You need something to eat tomorrow," he said pointing right at Curly, "and I have nothing to give you. But our good Father in heaven owns the cattle on a thousand hills. He can provide all our needs. All we need to do is ask Him."

Curly remembered what John had said the night they had tried raiding the kitchen. "You mean praying like the Lord's Prayer: 'Give us this day our daily bread'?"

"That's it exactly," said Mr. Müller with a gleam in his eye. "Most people don't really believe God answers prayer, but I do. He keeps His promises, and I wanted to prove it to everyone."

"What do you mean, prove it?"

"Good question, lad. Usually, when people need money to do mission work they go around begging for it and telling everyone exactly what they need. When someone gives the money, no one believes it's from God; they just think it came from some generous person."

"But didn't it?"

"Possibly so. But I wanted to show that *God* would respond to our prayers in a way that no one could confuse with someone else's generous heart. It's God who makes people's hearts generous, but as things usually go, people get the glory instead of God. So, from the very first, I set up an experiment. Do you know what it was?" he asked, leaning back in the rocker and waiting for Curly to respond.

"No, sir. I have no idea."

"I decided that I would never reveal any need to a person who could fill that need. I would only tell God. Then, if someone came along and answered the need by giving what I prayed for, it would *have* to be God who put it in the person's heart to give."

"Did it work?" Curly eagerly asked.

"Oh, yes, many times God has sent the exact amount of money or food we needed on the day we needed it. We seldom have any extra food, but we've never gone hungry." He got up out of his rocker and went to the table where he picked up a worn Bible.

"I'll let you in on the experiment," he said as he turned the pages of the Bible, holding it down where the candlelight could fall on it. "Here, listen to this from Matthew 21:21 and 22: 'Jesus answered and said unto them, Verily I say unto you, If ye have faith, and doubt not . . . all things, whatsoever ye shall ask in prayer, believing, ye shall receive.'

"Now, the fact is, Curly, we have no food in any of the orphan houses for tomorrow's breakfast, and I have no money with which to buy any, but we prayed and asked God for breakfast, didn't we—you and me? So now you'll see if God is faithful to His promise or not."

Curly sat on the bed with his mouth open. Could it really be true that there was no food at Ashley Downs?

"Oh, dear," said Müller suddenly, "it's after two o'clock. You had better run along to bed, now, Curly. You need your sleep."

The next morning, the "prayer meeting" in Mr. Müller's room seemed like a strange dream. But as Curly dressed, he remembered that there was no food for breakfast. He had come to feel that Ashley Downs was a safe place to live, even wishing from time to time that his sister—if he could ever find her—could live there. But if there was no food and no money, then any day the whole "experiment," as

Müller called it, could come to a crashing end. He decided he'd better hurry up and leave for London as soon as possible.

He was nearly late for breakfast and came skidding to his place at the table as Mr. Müller walked in. Plates and cups were on the tables as usual, but when George Müller raised his hand to pray, Curly noticed that his words were different. Instead of saying, "Dear Father, we thank you for what you *have given* us to eat this morning," he said, "Dear Father, we thank you for what you *are going to give* us to eat this morning." Then Müller continued, "Children, let us remain standing in silence at our places until God provides our food."

What was that? Had the experiment failed already? Was there really no food at Ashley Downs? Were all the children going to go hungry? What if no food came at all—today or tomorrow or the next day. Would Müller close down the place and send the children away on their own? Müller had said God was like a Father to the fatherless . . . but it looked to Curly like God was no more trustworthy than his own father had been.

Just then one of the schoolmasters came rushing in through a door near Curly's table and called to Mr. Müller. A strange man, dressed in workingman's clothes, stood in the doorway. When George Müller stepped to the door, the boy overhead the man say, "Mr. Müller? I'm the baker in Bristol, and last night I couldn't sleep. Somehow, I felt you might not have enough bread for breakfast, and the good Lord

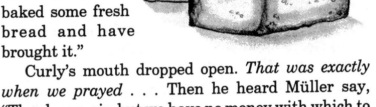

wanted me to send you some. So, I got up at two o'clock and baked some fresh bread and have brought it."

Curly's mouth dropped open. *That was exactly when we prayed . . .* Then he heard Müller say, "Thank you, sir, but we have no money with which to pay for it."

"Pay? I don't expect pay. How could I ask for money for bread God Almighty asked me to bake?"

Müller turned back into the dining room and said, "Children, we not only have bread, but the rare treat of fresh bread. Curly, could you and the other boys at your table go out and help unload it. Be sure to distribute equal amounts to each house."

As Curly was picking up the last armload of bread, a man came walking up the drive and said, "Say, son. Are you from the orphanage here?"

"Yes, sir," responded Curly.

"Well, I was on my way to town with all these cans of milk when my wheel broke just outside your gate. I have to get the weight off my wagon to repair it, but I don't want to dump all that fresh milk in the ditch. Do you think the orphanage could use any of it?"

Curly couldn't believe his ears. Maybe Mr. Müller was right. Maybe God was a *good* Father to the fatherless after all.

Chapter 10

Will the Boiler Blow?

T HE "BREAKFAST FROM HEAVEN," as George Müller called it, impressed Curly. Mr. Müller had often told stories after the meals about how God was caring for the children of Ashley Downs, but for the first time Curly really paid attention.

It was George Müller's practice to report to the children and to other people how God had provided for their needs *after* God had done so. In fact, Mr. Müller wrote reports and even traveled around the country speaking to churches and other groups of Christians about how money came in at the right moment. "How else will people know the experiment is working?" he would say. "I must show them how faithful God is. But I don't go out begging for money. I tell *God* our needs; I tell *people* how God provides."

Then one Friday afternoon in November, Mr. Müller did report a need before God answered. "This is an emergency that no human can fill," he announced at lunch. "So I can tell you about it *before* God answers. I am asking all you children to pray.

"It seems the boiler of the furnace in House Number One has suddenly started to leak. It is a very bad leak, and winter is coming soon. If we don't repair it, the heat will fail, and the little children will get cold. What's worse, if the boiler should go dry, it could blow up. I know our loving Heavenly Father would not want his little children to suffer, so we must pray that He will help us make the repair."

He then went on to explain that a brick wall surrounded the furnace making it impossible to replace or repair the boiler without tearing down the wall. Such a big project would take several days to complete, and if the weather were cold, the small children living in that house could not keep warm.

"We have scheduled the repairs for next Wednesday," he explained. "But, as you can see," and he pointed out the window, "a storm is coming. This north wind has picked up a bitter bite. It feels like the beginning of winter is already upon us. So, I ask you to pray with me for two things: that God would change this cold north wind into a warm south wind and that He would give the workmen a mind to work so the job can be completed quickly."

That was Friday. Saturday and Sunday the cold wind blew harder. Curly felt as if he were at a soccer game wishing his team could win but fearing—after seeing the size and skill of the other team—there was no chance.

Monday and Tuesday were no better. In fact, by Tuesday night—the night before the work was scheduled to begin—the sky looked heavy with snow about to fall.

After supper that evening Curly's schoolmaster encouraged the boys to gather around and pray. Several did, but Curly didn't say a word. *How could God be a loving Father?* he thought. *Maybe He's no different than my old man—doing what He wants, when He wants, no matter who it helps or hurts.*

That night as the wind howled outside the windows of his dormitory, Curly's dreams were troubled by visions of his father. In his dream, it was Christmas Eve, and even though his father had come home drunk, he had a bag of peppermint sticks and passed one out to each of the children. But as he staggered round the kitchen, he tripped over the broom that his little sister had left out. His father roared with anger and grabbed the peppermints  back from each of the children and threw them in the stove.

Curly awoke just enough to realize that it had only been a dream . . . or was it a dream? He knew that he wasn't back home, but the dream made him feel just like he had felt many times when he was little and his father had come home drunk. Finally, he went back to sleep, uncertain whether the dream was a memory of something that had actually happened or just something his mind had made up while he slept.

In the morning, Curly was awakened by shouts. Boys were hopping up and down by the windows and pointing outside. Forgetting the dream, he scurried over to where the boys were throwing open the windows. The sun was shining and the wind had shifted, coming now from the south. It was blowing so warmly and softly that it felt like spring instead of the beginning of winter.

The whole orphanage was abuzz with excitement as the workmen arrived with a wagon of tools and supplies. At breakfast, George Müller thanked the Lord for the weather as well as for the food. "He is a faithful Father," he reminded the children, "especially for those who have no father."

But for some reason, Müller's words today made Curly feel resentful. Somehow, the more of God's goodness he saw at Ashley Downs, the more angry he became about his own life—an orphan at only six years old, the son of a mean father who had beat him and the rest of the family and then killed himself with drink. Unpleasant memories of his father that he had forgotten for years were coming back to him more and more frequently, as if they had all happened yesterday.

One was particularly vivid. His mother had been so sick that she couldn't get out of bed. She had asked Curly to keep the fire going, but Curly had forgotten. When his father came home late and drunk, he hit his mother while she was in bed, for letting the house get cold.

Curly tried to forget those memories on that bright November day. He was assigned to make sure that the younger children who lived at House Number One didn't go near the dangerous construction area or get in the way of the workmen going back and forth to their wagon for tools and supplies.

The work began quickly as the men broke open the brick wall with their sledgehammers and pry bars, but on several occasions Curly was startled by one or another of the girls who ran past. If a girl had blonde hair and was about the right age, the same thought kept flashing through his mind: *Maybe that's my sister.* Of course, when he looked more closely, the girl never was, but it got him to thinking. *If I ever find her just livin' on the street or with some family who ain't good to her, I'm gonna bring her here.*

By noon, the workmen had found the part of the boiler that was leaking. "I think we can rivet a new plate on here and have it ready to fire up in no time," said the foreman to George Müller when he came by to see how the work was going. "But it'll take another day to rebuild that wall."

That afternoon the owner of the repair company came by and asked the workmen if they could work late and come early the next morning to finish the

work before
cold weather returned.

"We've been talking," said the lead repairman.
"We'd rather work all night." The other repairmen
nodded. "These children need the heat, so we might
as well keep going."

Curly couldn't believe his ears. In his excitement,
he ran to find Mr. Müller. "Guess what, Mr. Müller?"
he said when he found the old man. "God answered
the other part of your prayer. Those repairmen have

'a mind to work.'"

"Well, you may be right, Curly. It seems to me that they've been doing a very good job, and the work is coming along quite nicely."

"No, no. It's more than that. They just volunteered to work all night so they can finish the job before the cold returns."

That night in bed Curly wrestled with conflicting thoughts and feelings. Maybe God *was* a loving Father as George Müller said. He had to admit that God certainly seemed to answer Mr. Müller's prayers. *But He's not* my *Father*, thought Curly. *God might help Mr. Müller, but He's never helped me. I better play it safe and go back to London and get that money. Then I can take care of myself!*

Chapter 11

Leaving

BY NOW CURLY HAD SAVED nearly two pounds and he figured that would be enough to get him back to London. He had no idea how much a ticket would cost to travel by public coach, but he would ride as far as possible and walk the remaining miles.

At midnight—nearly a year after he'd come to Ashley Downs—Curly crept out of his dorm room and hurried down the lane toward the large gates of Ashley Downs. It was cold and dark but not completely black. The moon was behind the clouds.

When Curly reached the gates, they were locked. No problem. He quickly hauled himself up and over the top and was climbing down the outside when a voice said, "Well, well. And where are you headed this late, young man?"

Curly froze, clinging to the gate. It was Mr. Müller's familiar voice. "Nowhere," grunted Curly, not knowing how else to answer.

"Certainly you weren't coming out on a night like this to escort me home from town. Come on down here and show me who you are."

Curly dropped to the ground, realizing for a second time that Mr. Müller had caught him, but he could escape by running if he wanted to. Instead, he turned and faced the old man.

"It's too dark for me to make out who you are, so speak up and give me your name."

No sense lying. "It's me, sir, Curly Roddy."

"So, what are you up to? Do you have a friend somewhere you are wanting to visit, Mr. Roddy?"

"No, sir."

"Then what are you doing?"

"I'm leaving, sir."

"Leaving? You don't like it here at Ashley Downs?" Müller made no move to stop Curly as he got out a key and unlocked the gate.

Curly swallowed. "It's not that, sir. I just want to make my way on my own."

"Well, as I recall, you've tried that before, so you know what you're in for. I can't imagine that living on the streets is better than living here, but if you want to go, you can go. This isn't a prison, you know. You could leave during the day . . . and in your own clothes, I might add. That is an orphanage uniform you have on there, isn't it?"

Curly looked down at the blue coat and brown pants. "Yes, sir. I didn't mean to be stealing it."

"I should hope not. But it's yours; you can wear it if you want to. However, your street clothes might suit you better in the outside world. Why don't you come on with me and spend the night. Tomorrow, you can get your old clothes, enjoy a good breakfast, and leave by daylight." Mr. Müller went on through the gate and held it open for Curly.

Curly stood there debating with himself whether he should wait till morning or leave right then. For some reason he believed Mr. Müller—that he would be free to leave in the morning if he wanted to. The old man had never deceived him. And yet, going back felt like giving up. He had saved and planned so long. But Müller was standing there with the gate open, waiting for him; with a sigh Curly went back through the gate and followed Müller to the dorm.

"You run on up to bed now, and don't tell anyone about our little adventure tonight. In the morning, if you still want to go, come see me. Goodnight, now. I have some hard praying to do."

Curly didn't say anything. He was afraid that Mr. Müller's "hard praying" might be for God to keep him from leaving, and since God answered George Müller's prayers so often, that was scary. But Curly was determined to let nothing stop him.

The next morning he went immediately to George Müller's quarters and knocked on his door. "Well?" said the kind old man.

"I want to leave," said Curly.

"I thought as much, so I had Mrs. Bentley get your old clothes out of storage. They don't look too shabby." Mr. Müller eyed Curly in a way that made the boy think that he knew that the clothes had been purchased with stolen money.

Curly took the clothes, suddenly feeling very guilty.

"See you at breakfast," Mr. Müller said as Curly hurried back down the hall. He decided that he wouldn't put on his street clothes until after breakfast. It would save him from having to explain to everyone what he was doing.

After breakfast, Mr. Müller called Curly forward.

Oh, no, thought Curly. *What's he doing? Is he going to punish me in front of the whole house?* But he got out of his seat and walked to where Mr. Müller stood.

"Children," said Mr. Müller, "You all know Curly Roddy. He's been with us for nearly a year, but today he's going to be leaving us. We are going to miss you, Curly, and we want you to know that you are always welcome here. But before you go, we want to pray with you."

He put his hand on Curly's head and then began: "Dear Father, You love Curly even more than I can love him, and so I ask You to care for him wherever he goes and in whatever he does. Protect him from sin and sickness and provide what he needs . . ."

Curly couldn't believe how sincerely the old man was praying. George Müller wasn't trying to convince him not to leave, he was blessing him, praying for the best for him. The boy was so surprised that he opened his eyes and looked up at Müller. Large tears were streaming down the man's wrinkled face as he prayed, and suddenly Curly realized that he was loved, really loved, by someone. It was the biggest shock of his life.

The boy didn't even hear the rest of the prayer. Instead, all he could hear running through his mind were Müller's words about God being a loving Father. *If I had a real father like Mr. Müller,* Curly thought, *then maybe I could believe that God was a loving Father, too.* It didn't occur to Curly that in the loving care of George Müller, God had provided him with a loving, earthly father . . . but he was walking away from that gift.

Suddenly, the prayer was over, and Curly was surprised when Müller gave him a big hug. "Let's give Curly a cheer," he suggested.

The whole dining room erupted with, "Hip, hip, hurrah! Hip, hip, hurrah! Hip, hip, hurrah!"

Curly walked away from Ashley Downs that morning with strange, conflicting feelings. On the one hand, he felt free, headed for adventure! After living on the streets for six years, all that schoolwork and kitchen duty and bedtimes at the orphanage had felt very confining. On the other hand, Ashley Downs was the only home he'd known for years, even more pleasant than his childhood. He'd made some good friends and—he had to admit it—they were people who loved him.

But then he thought of the stash of money just waiting for him behind that loose rock in the warehouse—fifteen hundred pounds, minus whatever Spuds managed to spend before the police came. Why, with that much money, he wouldn't have to pray and wait and wonder whether God was going to answer his prayers like He answered Mr. Müller's.

Pushing down the guilt feelings that nagged at him for planning to keep the orphanage's money, Curly kept on walking.

Chapter 12

Treasure's End

CURLY ARRIVED IN LONDON late on the day before Christmas. It had taken him almost a week, by farmer's wagon and public stagecoach, walking on mild days to help save his money. Now a light snow was falling that brightened the otherwise dingy city and made the afternoon cheerful.

Curly walked past St. George's Church—just for old time's sake. Some people were standing on the steps singing Christmas carols. Someone was playing a trumpet, another a horn, and two more were keeping time with tambourines.

He stopped with other passersby and joined in as the carolers encouraged the listeners to sing along with "We Wish You a Merry Christmas." Then he hurried along to the warehouse.

As he approached, a light shone from inside and he noticed the large front door was open and a wagon was sitting in the entrance. Two men were unloading large sacks of something—maybe flour, Curly guessed—and stacking it in the warehouse. Curly walked past on the other side of the street so as not to attract any attention. He continued until he was nearly a block away and could just see the front of the warehouse.

There, he waited until the driver pulled his horse and wagon out of the entrance and drove back down the street.

Within a few minutes, someone came out of the warehouse and closed the front door, but it was getting so dark Curly could not see if the man shut himself in the building or locked the door from the outside and left.

Curly retraced his steps, trying to see if light showed through the two small windows high in the front wall of the warehouse. No light was visible, but that didn't guarantee anything. The man could have carried the light to the back part of the building where it couldn't be seen from the street.

Cautiously, the boy moved closer and finally crossed the street, studying the windows and the crack around the door for any signs of light. At any moment he was ready to pretend to be casually walking by . . . or run, if necessary, should someone open the door.

How stupid of me, Curly thought. *All I have to do is look for tracks in the snow. That will show me if the man went back through the door or walked away*. Sure enough, there in the snow, almost blue in the fading light of the late afternoon, was a set of footprints leading up the street in the same direction the wagon had gone.

Curly's heart beat faster. He was so close to the treasure. He looked both ways to make sure no one saw him, then he ducked down the narrow passage between the warehouse and the building next door. He had come this way so often when he was living with Spuds that he knew each step: the place where rain water had washed a ditch in the ground, the steel trapdoor to the warehouse's unused coal bin, the stack of old lumber partially blocking the passage, even the step up at the far end.

Curly peeked around the corner. Everything looked the same—the familiar rain barrel, the rubbish heap—and no one was around. He hadn't expected anyone; the back entrance to the building was seldom used except by Spuds and himself, and the other buildings in the neighborhood with doors opening onto the narrow alley had no watchmen staying inside.

Curly proceeded, noting with relief that there were no tracks in the thin layer of snow. Apparently, no new watchman had taken Spuds' place ... at least not one who used the back door.

Suddenly, the passageway seemed to explode right beside Curly. There was a loud screech and several cans came tumbling down off the rubbish heap. Curly jumped back, ready to run for safety.

Then he saw that it was only a cat escaping down the alley. He stood there, his legs so weak that he almost sank to the ground. *Maybe I should come back tomorrow in the daylight*, he thought, shaking. *It'll be Christmas, and no one will be around.*

But then there was the question of where he was going to spend the night. He was almost out of money, and after the long trip from Bristol, he was very tired and didn't want to have to find a dustbin to sleep in. Besides, it was getting colder.

As he proceeded toward the back door, he considered spending the night in the warehouse. But that was too risky. It was one thing to get caught sleeping where you shouldn't. Someone might yell at you or hit you as he chased you off, but if he were caught in the warehouse with all that money, he would go to prison. The police would know immediately where it came from.

He needed to get the money and get away from the warehouse for good.

He tried the door, but it was locked. That wasn't unusual; it was supposed to be locked. He moved a few feet away and lifted the rock where Spuds always kept the key. A wave of reassurance flooded over Curly when his fingers found it in the cold earth. It was rusty and dirty, but it was there.

However, when he tried it in the lock, it wouldn't even go in, let alone turn. In a panic, Curly tried jamming the key at the hole again and again, but it was no use. Finally, he calmed himself and looked more closely. Someone had changed the lock. No wonder the old key wouldn't fit.

He had to think. There must be another way into the building. He studied the lock in the failing light; maybe he could break in, but that didn't look hopeful. He thought about trying to force the front door or climb through one of the front windows, but that was too risky. Anyone coming down the street might see him.

There had to be another way!

Curly "thought" his way around the building, imagining it from every angle. *I might be able to get up on the roof, but what good would that do? There's no way in from there.* And then he remembered the steel trapdoor to the coal bin. He had no idea why the warehouse had a coal bin. There was no furnace, and the little stove Spuds used didn't take that much coal. But still, it was there. Maybe the building had been something else at one time and needed a furnace.

He ran back around the building and up the narrow passage to where the steel trapdoor was set into the side of the warehouse wall. There was no lock on it, just a piece of old wire twisted to hold the door closed. Curly undid the wire and pulled on the door, but it had been closed for so many years that the hinges had rusted tight.

He braced his legs and pulled harder. Still it wouldn't budge. Finally, he gave up and went looking for something to pry the door open. In a few minutes, he found a stick and returned to use it as a lever. With a creaking groan, the door slowly swung open.

Inside, there was only blackness. Curly could not see anything. He poked the stick through the opening and felt around on the floor inside. Then, using the stick to steady himself, he climbed through the hatch. There, except for the square of dim light behind him, he was in total blackness.

He took a step forward and ran into something. He felt with his hands and discovered a wall of barrels higher than he could reach and extending in both directions. There was only a narrow passage between the barrels and the outside wall of the warehouse.

The boy crept along in one direction knowing that at some point the stack of barrels must end. It did, but his way was blocked with wooden crates that were stacked tight against the wall preventing him from going any farther.

He retraced his steps and tried going in the other direction, but the passage grew narrower until he couldn't squeeze himself through any farther. In this direction, the barrels were stacked closer and closer to the wall. A terrible vision of him getting stuck passed through Curly's mind. *They might never find me back here*, he thought.

He went back the other way until he came to the crates. There, with much difficulty, he found hand holds that enabled him to climb. Higher and higher he struggled until he came to the roof of the warehouse. Between the top of the boxes and the roof there was enough space to crawl over the boxes. It was easier climbing down the other side since the boxes weren't stacked straight but like stair steps, and soon he reach the open area of the warehouse.

He worked his way across the floor like a blind man, hands out in front of him, taking little shuffling steps so as not to trip and fall over something.

In this manner, he proceeded in the direction where he remembered Spuds' small living quarters had been. All the while, he worried whether he could find his way back out. Could he find the right pile of crates to climb up, over, and out?

Suddenly, he was struck a terrible blow right in the face. He staggered back as lights flashed in his head. He waved his arms in front of him and found that he had crashed into a post that supported the roof of the building. Somehow, with both arms out, he had held them wide enough for them to go on either side of the post as he walked smack into it.

He was recovering from the shock, when he realized where he was. This was the post that stood at the edge of Spuds' living space! A few steps to the right should be the old stove, and beyond it, near the wall, should be Spuds' bed.

Curly sidestepped, waving his arm in the dark until his hand clanged into the stovepipe. It made a terrible but comforting racket. And, it was still warm. It felt good on the boy's hands. He worked his way around the stove and proceeded through the gloom toward the bed.

One more step and I ought to be there, he thought. He took another step and another, but there was no bed, and he finally bumped into the wall. The bed was gone. Fear seized him. *If they've removed the bed, maybe they cleaned out this whole area and found the loose stone in the wall. Maybe they got the money!*

In a panic, Curly began feeling the stones in the wall. Back and forth his hands worked, dislodging bits of old mortar and sand from between the stones. Curly could smell the dust of the place that he was stirring up, but he could not find the loose stone.

Then, with relief, he was sure he had found it. It was in the right place, and his fingertips could not feel any mortar around it. He pulled on the stone as he had seen Spuds do, but it would not move. He pulled harder until his fingernails tore but without any luck.

Should he go back and get the stick he'd used to pry open the coal bin door? Maybe he could use it to work the stone loose. Other worries filled his mind: *Maybe I've got the wrong stone. Maybe they found the money and sealed this stone back in place, and I can't feel the new mortar.*

Finally, he gave up. It was hopeless. Going back

for the stick and returning felt impossible. He began to panic. He wanted out of the warehouse more than he wanted the money. He had to get out before he was caught. *How long have I been in here?* he wondered. *Maybe it's Christmas morning already!*

He began to head toward the other side of the warehouse, hoping that he could find the right stack of crates to climb over when his shins crashed into a low table, tipping it over and sending him tumbling to the floor. It was all Curly could do not to jump up and start running, but his mind told him that would be crazy.

"Sit still and calm down," he told himself in a whisper. "No one is in here. No one knows you're in here." He forced himself to stay seated on the floor and count to ten. As he did so, his hand came across something long and round and smooth but not cold or heavy like a pipe. *It's a candle,* realized Curly. He patted around further on the floor. His hands hit a tin cup, a spoon, and a few other items that must have been on the table, and then they came upon a small paper box.

It held matches, and they rattled when Curly shook them. He pulled one out and struck it on the floor.

The flare of the flame almost blinded him, and it took a minute before his eyes adjusted and he could light the candle. Then he stood up and looked around.

Apparently, *someone* had been staying there. The person had moved Spuds' bed. There was a crate with some food in it and some old clothes, but those things didn't interest Curly. He turned toward the wall and saw that he had been working on the right stone . . . at least the one behind which he remembered Spuds hiding his things.

But if it was the right stone, why wouldn't it budge? When he examined it more closely, however, his heart leaped. The reason the stone wouldn't move was that a wooden peg had been wedged into its

right edge. The peg held the stone firmly. Curly went back to the upended table and retrieved the spoon. He worked its handle behind the peg and soon popped it out.

He put the candle down, paying no attention that it was on its side and the wax was melting while the flame got bigger. He pulled on the stone, and this time it moved. It was heavier than he had imagined, and he had to brace himself as it slid out. He put it down and grabbed the candle and looked into the opening.

There was a leather bag that *looked* like the one that had been in the money case. Curly pulled it out slowly, almost reverently. Would the money be there? He was shaking with excitement as he opened the bag and reached in.

His fingers closed around first one, then another and another stack of paper pound notes.

The money was still there.

Chapter 13

Christmas for Somebody's Sister

CURLY PULLED OUT A WAD of paper money. He put it back and pulled out a handful of coins . . . a few were even gold. *I'm rich*, he thought. The realization caused him to break into a heavy sweat.

He had an urge to take the money and flee the warehouse as fast as he could run, but he told himself it was better to put things back the way he found them. *No one else knew this money was here, but it would be dumb to announce that I was here looking for something. With that hole in the wall, the police might even figure out what was in it.*

He put the candle down. Then, realizing there was no way to lift the heavy stone with one hand, he reluctantly set the money bag down and replaced the stone in the wall. He righted the table and arranged the things back on it as he thought they might have been, then picked up the money bag.

The interior of the warehouse loomed large and dark, and his small light extended only a short distance, but once he blew it out, he would plunge into complete blackness—*and crash into things again, maybe even drop the money*, he worried. Then an idea came to him, and he picked his way carefully toward the back door. *Maybe I can open that lock from the inside*, he thought.

Sure enough, stuck in the lock from the inside was the key. Curly tried turning it, and it opened easily. He left the door open and took the candle back to the table. When he blew it out, the room was as dark as he remembered, but behind him was the faint light from the open door to guide him.

As he closed the door behind him, he took the key and locked the door from the outside, then tossed it into the alley as though someone had accidentally dropped it there. Around to the side of the warehouse, he closed the coal bin hatch.

He'd done it. He was out of the building with the money in hand!

An hour later he sat in the Cracker Box Inn with a big bowl of chicken soup in front of him. He had taken a small amount of money from the bag and stuffed it into his pocket so he wouldn't have to show the bag to anyone when he paid for things. He had arranged a way to tie the bag to the inside of his coat out of sight.

The hot meal tasted good, and he had already paid for a room at the Wayfarer's Boarding House down the street. How many times had he walked past there wishing he could have a warm bed for even one night? Now he could stay there a week, a month, for as long as he wanted! Life was sweet. *And tomorrow is Christmas*, he reminded himself.

He tried to remember Christmas as a young child at home with his mother and brothers and sisters. There were bad memories, but there had also been better times: Christmas carols sung around the fire, Mother telling the Christmas story, baked apples, plum pudding. And once, he remembered, they had even eaten a Christmas goose.

In spite of his good fortune, he felt sad that he had no family to be with at this Christmas season. He began imagining how the children at Ashley Downs might be celebrating Christmas. They had been practicing parts for a play before he left. He would have been one of the shepherds guarding the sheep on the hillside when the angels announced Jesus' birth. *I wonder who took my part*, he thought.

His dreaming was interrupted by a towheaded kid—a couple of years younger than himself—who began singing Christmas carols on the other side of the room, near the bar. The child was dirty and skinny and sang with a thin, pinched voice. When the song ended, the child removed a greasy cap and went from table to table to receive donations.

Though Curly had a pocketfull of coins, he wasn't going to put any money in the cap. But when the child came to his table, he was surprised to discover that she was a girl. He looked closely at the smudged face and saw that it wasn't all dirt. The girl had a black eye and red, rough patches on her cheeks from recent frostbite. *She's been sleeping outside*, he thought.

He dug out a sixpence and tossed it into the girl's cap. A big smile spread over her thin face, and suddenly she reminded him of his sister. He squeezed his eyes shut to block out the sight of her. *Why does every towheaded girl remind me of my little sister?* When he opened his eyes again, the girl had returned to the bar and had begun to sing another carol.

Curly spooned the last of the soup into his mouth and tried to concentrate on a vision of his sister. She hadn't really looked like this girl, but then he couldn't really remember what she looked like anymore. Every time he tried, the image melted into the girl singing the Christmas carols . . . or the little girl with

129

the gray-shawled woman from St. George's Church
. . . or one of the girls from Ashley Downs.

He had lost his sister, and now his memory of her was escaping him as well.

When the young singer came around again with her hat in hand, no one put money into it, but Curly knew the kind of life she was living. He had lived such a life, too! He knew no one should have to sleep on the streets and beg for food. And besides, she was *somebody's* sister.

He reached into his pocket again, intending to give her enough to buy food for several days and maybe a place to sleep. When he looked up, she was smiling again, eagerly awaiting his gift. But he realized it wouldn't really help her. In a few days the money would be gone, and she would be as miserable as ever. *She may not even survive the winter,* he realized.

"Come with me," he said, and led her outside where the lamp hanging beside the door of the Cracker Box shone on her face. "I've got money," he said eagerly. "It's enough for both of us. You can live with me."

A frightened look came over her face. Possibly others had made a similar offer and then treated her meanly. Curly could see that she was about to run. "No, wait," he said, thinking fast. There had to be a better plan, one that would last, one that would give her a home, people to love and take care of her. She needed more than he could offer, even with his money.

"What you need is Ashley Downs," he blurted out.

"What?" The young girl looked at him suspiciously.

"I said, you need to live in an orphanage like Ashley Downs."

The girl snorted. "Orphanages are for rich children, not for the likes o' me. I guess you don't know nothin'," she said and started to turn away.

"Not Ashley Downs." Curly reached out and put his hand gently on her shoulder. "Mr. George Müller built it for kids just like you . . . and me. I'm . . . I'm going there tomorrow," he stammered, hardly realizing what he was saying, "and I'll take you with me, if you want. It can be your Christmas present."

"I ain't had a Christmas present since my ma died," the skinny girl said as a little smile melted her hard features. "But why would they take us in?"

"I used to live there." Curly was thinking fast, realizing what he had to do. "And—and I've got a lot of money that I'm supposed to deliver to Mr. Müller. He's a very kind man . . . like a father, and, besides, he invited me to come back."

The girl studied Curly's face for a moment, trying to decide whether to believe him or not. Finally, she said, "All right. I'll go with you if you think it is such a good place."

"Oh, you'll find it much better than the streets of London. I can assure you of that. Now, let me take you back inside the Cracker Box and get you something to eat."

While the girl hungrily devoured a hunk of bread and a bowl of chicken soup, Curly thought about what he had promised. *I wouldn't have to return the money,* he reasoned. After all, this was his one big chance to be rich. *I could deliver the girl and then leave again without ever mentioning the money.* But the longer he watched the dirty blonde girl hungrily spoon hot broth into her mouth, the more he realized that the money didn't belong to him. It belonged to the orphanage to be used for children just like this girl . . . and himself.

It is *a good place to live*, he admitted to himself. *Maybe . . . just maybe . . . I'll stay, too.*

More About George Müller

GEORGE MÜLLER WAS BORN in Kroppenstadt, Prussia, on September 27, 1805. His father had high hopes for him and paid for his education in the town of Wolfenbüttell during his teen years, hoping that George would become a Lutheran minister. But young Müller was an irresponsible playboy, frequently getting in trouble for drinking, gambling, and running up big debts. For such reckless behavior, George even ended up in jail.

However, when Müller was twenty years old and attending the university in Halle, a friend convinced him to attend a prayer meeting and Bible study in a private home. There Müller gave his life to Jesus and, before long, decided to become a missionary. This made his father angry, since the old man had hoped that, as a clergyman, George would be able to support him in his old age, so Father Müller refused to give his permission.

Without his father's formal permission, the German missionary societies would not accept George, so he went to London, England, in 1829 to train with the Society for Promoting Christianity among the Jews.

Ill health forced him to move to the country. There he joined the Plymouth Brethren and became a preacher at Ebenezer Chapel in the town of Teignmouth. Müller was such an effective preacher that the little congregation grew from eighteen members to 227 in under three years.

It was while he was here that he came to the conviction that the money he needed to live on should be supplied by the Lord through prayer alone. He stopped the practice of charging rent for people to sit in the church pews and refused a personal salary. Instead, he relied entirely on gifts from Christians. It was a bold experiment in its day, but God blessed.

In 1835, Müller opened an orphanage in the city of Bristol for common children. At that time, only the children of wealthy or important families were accepted in England's few orphanages. If relatives did not take in the children of the poor when thier parents died, the children were left on the streets or sent to cruel work houses.

This was the period in English history about which Charles Dickens wrote the novel, *Oliver Twist*. In fact, at one point (some time later) Charles Dickens visited George Müller's orphanages to investigate whether the children were being well-treated. Dickens went away entirely reassured.

Müller's objective for establishing the orphanages was twofold: He wanted to care for needy children, and he wanted to prove to the world that God will supply anyone's needs who will trust only in Him and pray.

When the house in Bristol became too crowded for the space where it was located, Müller purchased some out-of-town property, known as Ashley Downs, and built a larger home there. The move to Ashley Downs in 1849 and subsequent construction of four more large homes over the next twenty years was accomplished by a series of dramatic miracles of God's provision. Once the five great houses at Ashley Downs were completed, they were home for two thousand children at a time.

The drama of God's miraculous provision of everything from food to money for construction was an almost daily occurrence at the orphan homes. Again and again money or supplies arrived with only minutes to spare before the children sat down at table. Miracles of that sort retold in this book are only a sample of hundreds of such incidents.

Müller's demonstration of God's provision was not confined to orphanages. He also founded the Scriptural Knowledge Institution which trained and supported missionaries as well as encouraged the education of children and adults around the world. And his principles of trusting God had an impact on other mission efforts. In fact, at the age of seventy, Müller set out with his second wife on a worldwide mission, which lasted seventeen years. His witness to the prayer-hearing God of the Bible prompted the establishment of orphanages based on similar faith principles in many lands.

During his life, which ended on March 10, 1898, Müller housed, educated, and trained over ten thousand boys and girls. He managed nearly one and a half million pounds in money contributed for the orphan work. But Müller was also very generous with his own money. In fact, he gave away almost nine-tenths of all money given directly to him, and at his death his total estate, including all furniture, was valued at only 160 pounds.

For Further Reading

Bergin, George Frederic, *Ten Years After: A Sequel to The Autobiography of George Müller* (London: J. Nisbet & Co., Ltd.; Bristol: Scriptural Knowledge Institution, 1911).

Garton, Nancy Wells, *George Müller and His Orphans* (Westwood, N. J.: Fleming H. Revell Company, 1963).

Miller, Basil, *George Müller: Man of Faith and Miracles* (Minneapolis, Minn.: Bethany House Publishers, 1941).

Müller, George, *Autobiography of George Müller* (London: J. Nisbet; Bristol: Bible and Tract Warehouse, 1905).

Steer, Roger, *George Müller: Delighted in God!* (Wheaton, Ill.: Harold Shaw Publishers, 1981).

Stocker, Fern Neal, *George Müller, Champion of Orphans* (Boise, Idaho: Pacific Press Publishing Association, 1986).